THE JOURNEY

HEATH WILLIAMS

The Journey
Copyright © 2023 by Heath Williams

ISBN
978-1-961250-24-6 (Paperback)
978-1-961250-25-3 (eBook)
978-1-961250-23-9 (Hardcover)

THE JOURNEY

Table of Contents

KIND WORDS

"*The Journey* absolutely lives up to its name. Intriguing from the onset, this tale of a troubled life will carry you on a roller coaster ride full of twists and turns. Joe's story shows not only his own vulnerability, but ours as well. My heart was touched and my faith was renewed. Yours will be too."

~Jamie Hughes,
founder of Writing for Well-Being.

"For the very first time, the journey to life in Christ is clarified in story – laymen terms relative to real life. The Journey is a plight into relationship with Christ in such a profound well-written manner that it's sure to win souls for Jesus Christ…. I eagerly await the sequels to Joe's journey!!!!"

-STACEY GLOVER,
FLOW FELLOWSHIP INTERNATIONAL.

Abyss — a place of demons…

Luke 8:30,31 NASB

*"And Jesus asked him, 'what is your name?"
And he said, 'Legion'; for many demons had
entered him. They were imploring Him not to
command them to go away into the abyss."*

For anyone brave enough to ask….

Is this really it?
Is this how it's supposed to be?
Is this what God had in mind?

Forward

The Journey is one of the most prolific literary masterpieces ever penned. Heath Williams is a venerable giant in the field of evangelism; as the mind of Christ and heart of God are explicitly revealed through his creative genius. As his first released work of literature, Williams graciously presents the world a priceless treasure and intricately weaves the Gospel message without pungency. *The Journey* graciously and successfully integrates God's word into every aspect of Joe's personal plight and spiritual expedition and His presence is felt on every page.

Truly, Joe's weaknesses later render a formidable strength never dreamed or envisioned. Remarkably, *The Journey* is a tale of amazing romance and love story as intimately disclosed through the courtship of Joe and his newfound love affair with God. Williams unearths some truths about Joe's life as seen through the eyes of Christ and his quandary quickly becomes every man's story. This exceptional read dispels judgment; as the message of grace and forgiveness resonates throughout the pages. Without question, *The Journey* is every man's book!

Heath Williams renders *The Journey* — a stupendous masterwork of brilliance that effectively sermonizes the Gospel and imaginatively conveys it to both the spiritually inept and the seemingly scholastic erudite. Such outstanding artistry far removes the confines surrounding the traditional platforms of church, and brings the pulpit home to one's chair, bed, study or designated reading peruse. Williams executes a stroke of genius as *The Journey* concludes with Joe picking up a pen and beginning to write. King David declared in Psalms 45:1a (KJV): "…my tongue is the pen of a ready writer." At journey's end, it is very refreshing to comprehend that Joe's journey is just beginning and the world is left sitting on the edge of its seat and excitedly awaits its continuance. Indeed, *The Journey* continues….

Bishop Stacy T. Glover, Presiding Prelate
FLOW Fellowship International Incorporated
Spartanburg, South Carolina

Introduction

Depression – The human, both in body and mind, can't go here on its own. It's not natural and it's not an instant arrival.

In fact, depression is so awful, let's not even use the word. (Let's just refer to it as 'D'. Same as its relatives, stress and anxiety, refer to them as 'S' and 'A'). D is a thief and a liar that robs us of everything good while we are on our journey through life. S and A help fuel D.

Again, we don't arrive at it, just the same as we don't just exit from it. D is a powerful scam artist. We are deep into it before we realize it. We usually don't even know that we had flirted with it. Then we are so engrossed that it's more 'comfortable' staying with it than trying to recall what we were like without it. It's literally and almost physically like living in a box; a cold, dark, black hell box, oozing with voices. D, the demon it is, whispers lots of bad things, like, *just stay here, it's okay. This is where you belong. It's always been this way. This is life – don't you know this? If you were smarter you would know this. What do you think you deserve anyway – you're alive aren't you — you have family — you have existence and routine…'*

This is depression.

That damn coward is the worst form of death because unfortunately, you still breathe. Again, there's no defined entrance and there's no clear exit. There's no memory of when we let him in.

Too many people are living with this enemy. He is in fact death to our life. He is a thief and a liar. He's impartial too. There's no socioeconomic or demographic boundaries. Too many people are in his lair at various stages. It's the most prevalent sickness on the planet.

BUT, he CAN be defeated!

Yes, he CAN!

Hope and desire are his kryptonite.

Are you brave enough to use them and squash him beneath your feet?

In the most ironic twist possible, D, is actually a launching point. You WILL conquer it. You WILL put him in his place — your past. AND, the knowledge gained grows you to a better you. AND, the path out of it turns into an accelerated joyride as long as you are brave enough to keep fueling yourself with Hope and Desire! Your 'fuel' may not be the same as everyone else's and that's ok. We may all have different 'fuel', but his kryptonite is same for all — Hope and Desire. This coupled with willingness to pursue change is more powerful than the scam! Even more awesome is the fact that pursuit of change is more valuable than the end result itself. We are not suddenly 'better' when we arrive at our desired change. The same as we don't suddenly wake up in 'D', we don't suddenly wake up in joy.

It's the journey we experience as we grow away from D that makes us who we want to be. And that journey is priceless!

Chapter 1

THE EDGE

The sun hovered above the mountains and the lake was peacefully still. The few stratus clouds that lingered provided a canvas for the colors painted by the early autumn sunset. The Appalachian Mountains seemed more vibrant and beautiful than ever as the sun began to slip behind them. The purple and orange sky slowly began to fade away as the day turned to dusk. The peacefulness of the lake added to the surrealness of the evening. It was the perfect ending to a perfect afternoon.

The stretch of lakefront belonged solely to mother nature and was void of any signs of alteration. An empty hillside was landlocked by thick forests that seemed to guard the grassy descent that led to the lakeshore where Joe was standing. The water sat motionless and appeared as glass as Joe gazed across it, toward the face of the mountains.

Joe tried to bask in the beauty of autumn's hues. Dogwoods offered their burgandy leaves while maples, sweetgums and hickory trees added their splendor. Green chlorophyll had released it's grasp on seemingly every leaf, allowing carotenoid compounds to splash the landscape with an array of orange and yellow.

Today had seemed to be what he needed; some time to relax. He was able to only steal a few hours from his busy schedule and he tried to make the most of his escape. The morning had been consumed with a few hours of work and then a rush to his youngest one's ballgame to watch her cheer. Except for the urging of his wife, he may had stayed home with the excuse of being too tired. She thought the time alone may be good for him, and her too. They both knew that he desperately needed a break, but Joe needed it a lot more than she could even imagine.

The hours had passed all too quickly and soon it was time to leave. Even before he had finished packing up his tackle box, it started coming back.... That awful, terrible problem he faced; the one that consumed him. The one that took the place of contentment, satisfacion and happiness. The problem that overshadowed a peaceful afternoon and robbed him of any joy that may had resulted from his fall furlough.

Joe stood perfectly still with tackle and rod in hand and gazed across the lake in the direction of the picturesque sunset, yet he was unable to absorb its beauty. The mountains seemed to draw him in closer as they beckoned to him. It had been several years since he had visited this special place that owned so much of his childhood. He thought about the seemingly endless days he spent playing in the nearby woods and all the hours fishing at practically the same spot that he was standing now. Scenes of his childhood flashed in his mind. Memories of being here as a kid propelled him to a better place. A place where things were simpler and happiness was plentiful. A point in time that he found himself longing for. A time long before his problem. He looked back at the field behind him and without effort, he could see kids playing. He saw everyone just as they were so many years before. He heard their laughter and their yells of excitement as they played. He saw them hiding in the tall weeds or sneaking from the edge of the woods to overtake their opponent. "TAG, got you! You're it", they yelled. The innocence of it all allowed Joe to temporarily escape his returning problem.

Maybe it was the unquenchable thirst for it to all be real, or perhaps the shiver from a cool autumn breeze that caused Joe to return to the present. Regardless, he was back. The sounds of crickets chirping and bullfrogs croaking reminded Joe that daylight was fading and he needed to get going. He tried to maintain some of the solitude he had experienced just minutes before that now suddenly seemed so distant.

How could it go away that quick? Joe thought. *Am I really that messed up? Why do I have this terrible problem?*

He tried to analyze his situation to console himself. If he could source the reason for his despondent gloom, then possibly he could try to overcome it.

Problems are tangible; something that can be fixed…. I don't have a problem, he decided…. *I have an empty hole.*

Joe's life felt completely void of meaning. What appeared to others as a normal, for Joe, had become an endless journey of emptiness. Joe felt that his life could not feel any worse.

The disappointment of not identifying a cause for his emptiness bothered him as much as the despairing aura itself. All he knew was that nothing made him happy anymore. Nothing provided joy like it used to; it seemed that everyday was just a drudgery. Regardless of the events or hurdles of each day, whether they should be perceived as good or bad, or easy or hard, life just clicked by day after day, void of much feeling of importance.

Overhead, the faint sound of an airplane interrupted Joe's analysis, causing him to look up. With head tilted back, he looked for the plane. His eyes slowly roamed, noticing that some stars were already visible in the early night sky. As Joe spotted the plane, he began to gaze past it as if to look further into the heavens.

God.... Joe thought, *are You out there?*

Then Joe's empty despair hinged on the verge of depression as he thought deeper and realized that he didn't have an empty hole. *I have an abyss*, Joe lamented.

He wished he could break down. Maybe that would make him feel better.

Just let it all out right here. Go ahead and sit down and have yourself a good cry, he thought.

Except he couldn't; the abyss didn't allow it. His sobs had no tears. Tears brought on by sadness are a healing ointment that Joe would love to induce. He is empty. Tears quit coming recently. At this point, sobbing would be an attempt to induce cleansing, relieving tears.

Yet, instead of fully entering depression's lair, he clung to the door jamb, but his grip was weakening. He realized he was weak and knew today's efforts were futile; his favorite season and his favorite activity was no remedy. He continued to search and analyze. When that didn't help, he reversed the progression and attempted to analyze in order to search. Confusion induced confusion. Sadness replaced despair.

I feel so alone!

The crickets chirped louder and the moan of the frogs sounded like a well-orchestrated chorus, conducted by mother nature herself. Despite his quest for answers, Joe wished that he could enjoy the sounds of the country, but the opportunity was vanished. With a disappointing shake of his head, Joe turned and headed across the field to the tree line at the edge of the woods he must cross to get back to his car.

After only a few minutes in the woods, he realized how quickly the day had turned dark. Even with a building sense of anxiety, Joe was able to sigh in admiration of the symbolism of his thought. With the next few steps, Joe began to swivel his head in search of the path he thought he knew. The one that would lead him back to his car. Joe stopped walking and stood perfectly still. A touch of fear set in. He tried to focus on finding the path but the pounding of his heart overtook his rational thought as fears escalated. With each breath getting faster, he looked up through the limbs of the trees engulfing him and realized he was completely lost.

* * * * * *

Joe is an average guy. In many ways, such as income and family, he's no different than most. On the surface all seems well, yet internally he's miserable. He still manages to have varied interests and hobbies, but like typical bread winners his age, he seldom has time for them and he's discovered that they no longer bring him much satisfaction. Nothing is satisfying anymore. Nothing brings happiness like it used to. He's fairly certain that it's not due to self-centeredness or greed or even boredom with life.

What? What is missing? Joe asks himself often. Even when it seemed that contentment was on the threshold, he still came up short.

It's like decorating for Christmas but without a family to enjoy it on Christmas morning, Joe had thought before. *The house looks nice. All red and green and shiny but not complete. A decorated house without a happy, loving family there to enjoy it.* That's how Joe's life feels. It's so empty. Unlike his analogical thoughts about a missing family at Christmas though, the missing part was not identified.

He often wonders if anyone else pursues an unknown goal like he does.

Am I the only one, he questions. *Do others feel alone? Without cause? Without purpose?*

He's assured himself that life should not feel so empty and wondered if his despair is due to a lack of purpose. Ironically, that revelation led to even deeper regret by questioning the very meaning of his existence.

I know I have responsibilities, but why am I even alive? What is the meaning of my existence, he pines. Perhaps discovering a deeper meaning would make things better. Perhaps purpose would lead to a joyful, contented, happy, and fulfilling life.

His empty hole; his missing purpose; his abyss, had started moving from sadness and despair to consuming and probably depression.

Something has to change. I can't go on like this.

Maybe the next few nights and days will help Joe discover the answers that will close his abyss.

* * * * *

Joe made it out of the woods. He had wondered in circles for approximately half an hour before realizing he was actually a lot closer to the opening where his car was parked than he thought. On the way home, he tried to get past the negative feelings he had and focus on the good part of the day; the tranquil sunset and fond memories. But the more he tried, the more he realized he couldn't fool himself.

I'm a Christian. Church is in the morning. Maybe I can pray and feel better…. And I'll really listen to the message. Maybe that will help me.

These thoughts seemed comforting to Joe as he made his way home. Despite his oppression, Joe looked forward to getting home to his wife and kids. He needed to feel the warmth of home and hear their voices. That would help him feel better, he hoped.

The next day came and went. Church was the usual; a nice message, a touch of emotion, and a sincere prayer.

CHAPTER 2

MONDAY

The two ladies had been crying uncontrollably. Their eyes were red and swollen. Others were there with them; some with blank stares; others sobbing. The sky was crystal clear except for only a small puffy cloud. Just above the lone tree Joe was standing under, the sun shown through bright.

If I step back one step, that big limb will shade me better. Joe thought as he wiped sweat from his forehead. Somewhere in the house a door shut. The sound awoke Joe. Or at least he thought it did.

Am I dreaming?

As Joe looked closer at the ladies and the gathering of friends and loved ones surrounding them, he wondered if someone had died. *Was anyone else coming from in the house?*

The ladies' blank expressions of extreme sadness turned to bewilderment, and then to shock. Whatever that man said to them caused one of the ladies to yell, "Why didn't you come when they told you?" "We sent word. Did you not believe?" She exclaimed. Despite her lament, she hugged him and cried more.

Joe looked down at his hands to convince himself that he's really seeing them. Details were beginning to come clearer and a sense of bewilderment started overcoming Joe. Also, a feeling of numbness; of euphoria maybe. Maybe it was the heat. The sun was hot. Joe's eyes seemed to dance along with the heat waves coming off the sand and rocks as he tried to observe his hands. Before he could focus, he realized, "this has to be real", he whispered to himself.

How could I observe so many details? Not in a dream, you can't, Joe convinced himself. *The sun, the crying ladies, the heat, the sweat. It's all real. I can even see the puffiness around those ladies' eyes,* Joe thought as he began to feel sad for them. *They had been crying so hard....*

There's that sound again. Someone keeps closing a door down the hall.

Wait, what door? Joe felt like he was about to black out. *I need to wake up....* Then a contrasting urge prompted him to think, *but, I don't want to.*

Joe gazed intently as his curiosity grew. *What is going on here?* He focused closer on the ladies again. *Why do those ladies look so puzzled now? They were so sad just seconds ago, and now... now they seem... puzzled and scared.*

"There's nothing to wake up from. This is real." Joe murmured to himself as he felt of his left sleeve with his right hand. *I know this is real. I feel the very detail of this cloth.* After a bewildered pause, he spoke a little louder, "WAIT". Then the thought, *what am I wearing?*

"Thomas, what's the matter?" "Are you having second thoughts about telling him we'll come here with him?"

Joe didn't look up.

"THOMAS". The voice said again.

Who is Thomas? Joe thought as he began to tremble in fear of what might be happening.

Why haven't I noticed I'm wearing some sort of..., of..., a robe.... A robe...? He almost said out loud as he looked down and then all around him. *That's what they all have on.*

Anguish welled up in Joe and in despair he started to shout. He thought that would surely wake him up.... He was convinced now that this was a dream.

Or is it?, He thought again.

Then it started to happen.

Before Joe could finish his thought, he was nudged from behind. He was reluctant to move but the throng of people that he now realized was surrounding him caused him to follow the order. A dozen or so people surrounded him. His thoughts seemed frozen as he walked. His sense of feeling and emotions seemed to vanish. He was feeling numb again. Feeling unreal.

Is it even sunny now? I can't focus good. I feel.... Thoughts and emotions started flooding back over Joe. More intense than before. Euphoria as it continued to happen. The crowd stopped moving and peered in the ladies direction.

WHAT? I can't believe it.... Joe thought in astonishment as he began to understand what he may be seeing. Joe wanted to speak his thoughts but couldn't. *Am I really seeing this? Am I really here?*

The people watched in utter amazement; with hopeful, bewildered expressions. The men around Joe began to bow. Some bowed on knees. Others fell flat on their faces. Joe could not feel anything physically;. just emotionally, but he could sense he was letting himself fall freely to the hard stony ground as he realized what was happening. It was really happening right there before his eyes.

As he reached the ground, he heard it.... "LAZARUS!!!!!... COME FORTH!!!!...."

Emotions he had never felt before swept over Joe. This was really happening. Joe was seeing it all first-hand. He was really seeing it. He didn't believe it but he really was seeing it. Every inch of his body tingled. He felt weightless. Like being in zero gravity, except he lay motionless on the ground. The left side of his face pressed against the sand and pebbles. His right arm lay flat with his elbow in a ninety degree bend and his hand flat, palm down in the sand.

Bound in cloth, he stumbled from the opening in the side of the hill. Lazarus came from the tomb. The Bible story of Lazarus unfolded right before Joe's eyes. Emotions coursing through him, Joe watched it all.

Somehow Joe managed to draw his fingers toward his palm. He didn't move his eyes from the dream before him but his peripheral sight saw his hand close as he formed a fist. The sand squeezed from between his fingers. He felt it. The flood of emotions continued. The feel of the sand and the rush of emotions further assured Joe that it was really happening. Fright, excitement, jubilation; every sense he had ever experienced was heightened greater than possibly humanly attainable.

Lazarus came from the dead. The story, just as he understood it from Sunday school as a child and a few times as an adult he may have heard it. The shift from Bible story to reality, in the flesh, before his very eyes was almost more than he could observe consciously.

Joe was still lying paralyzed on the ground. Fear, Joy, excitement; he wasn't sure what he felt. All he knew is he was seeing it for himself. The real story of Lazarus.

The ladies; *his sisters*, Joe thought, rushed to him. Joy gushed from them as they flooded Lazarus with kisses and hugs. Without uttering a sound, as if to not draw attention, like a child sneaking a piece of candy, Joe began to rise from the ground. He strained to see through his tear-filled eyes.

Some of the crowd ran to the reunion. Others stood in disbelief.

Joe finally completely stood up. He wanted to see more. Perhaps the revelation of being this close to Christ was too much for Joe to handle. Or perhaps the heart-pounding, adrenaline-pumping emotions did it. Or both. Regardless, he hit the ground again. This time with a frozen smile on his face and eyes wide open. Joe knew his expression must have looked funny, but yet he was unwilling to move or change quickly. He didn't want to wake up, if he was asleep.

Joe tried again to get up. He wanted to be sure he could see it all. The people were moving about more now and he didn't want to miss anything. *I want to see more*, he thought desiringly. He stumbled on wabbling legs for two or three steps.

Christ, was all he could think. Over and over the revelation of whose presence he was in echoed through his mind. Standing in euphoric amazement, Joe wanted to move closer. Without comprehension of taking any steps, he had moved closer. He now stood several steps behind Jesus. Over Christ's left shoulder he could see Lazarus begin to smile - his first expression since coming forth. As he began to smile, Joe began to sob more. Memories and revelations of his understanding of Jesus' love raced back to his thoughts as he realized Jesus simply smiled and gave a reassuring nod toward Lazarus as He turned to walk away. As Jesus turned, Joe thought he saw the side of Jesus' face.

Mental images were being confirmed or shaped with every detail that he tried to focus on. *His beard, His hair... His stature, His sandals....*

Again, Joe started to stumble. A multitude of emotions arose in him as his eyes yearned to observe more. Quickly, amongst the over-powering of his senses, he somehow had a feeling of guilt. Like a student mistakenly receiving an A they didn't deserve, he wondered if it was okay to stare. His mind raced to assure him that it was okay to soak up details and compare them with what he had always perceived to be the image of Christ. Awe-struck or maybe love-struck caused Joe to tremble all over. While taking mental images, he tried to simultaneously replay what he just saw; he was sure he had seen Jesus simply smile as He turned to walk on.

He just nodded and smiled, Joe thought.

Love as Joe had never experienced seemed to knock him back to the ground as he reflected on Jesus' nod. *Amazing love* absorbed Joe's thoughts while meeting the ground again.

The song rang loudly through his numbed thoughts. *Amazing love, how can it be, that you my King would die for me?* Over and over the words of the song he liked but knew very little of, echoed through him. Then, Joe realized more of the humbleness and intense love of his Savior as it seemed Jesus began to disappear from the crowd and the attention.

Just as he did after feeding the 5000. The way he went into the mountains to pray when everyone wanted to set him up as their king on earth.

Jesus simply smiled, nodded, and walked away. When the crowd realized he had begun leaving, many fell in his direction and started worshiping. Others shouted. Others cried hysterically and yet, somehow, others doubted. Regardless of what any of them thought, Joe knew no one realized it may be the last time some of them saw Him alive. *Well, on earth anyway,* he concluded. Then Joe realized he hadn't really got to see His face. He had only gotten a glimpse.

I want to see him!!!! Joe shouted to himself as he began getting his legs under him.

"Thomas".

Why are they calling me...? Thomas? A sense of reality began setting in Joe as he started thinking a little more clearly again. *Thomas? The doubter? Wait, they said earlier, 'was I having second thoughts about telling Him we would come here....' You mean Thomas, the doubter, encouraged Jesus to come to Lazarus? I will have to look this up when I...*

Joe wasn't sure how to finish his thought. *When I.... Wake up????*

"Come on. Rabbi is ready to move on", the voice said. Then Joe was nudged again to start walking.

Suddenly, the door opened and Joe awoke. It was over. Sadly, it was all over.

"Hey Paul Bunyan", Joe's wife said sarcastically, in reference to his story of getting lost in the woods two days before. "You gettin' up?"

Joe's eyes were wide open. He didn't move. His thoughts were if he was alive or not.

"Just woke the kids up", she said.

The door closing in the hall? Joe thought, still not moving. *The sound of a door closing during my dream. So I really was dreaming?* Joe exhaled as he concluded, *Of course I was.*

"Don't have time to fix breakfast", she said as she left the room. If Joe had been fully returned from the Holy Land, he may have caught the animosity in her voice.

Sensations of his dream were still present as Joe's feet touched the floor. He was completely awake. He had no desire to stretch or yawn, like he had not even been asleep. He looked at the clock, then out the window as if trying to confirm it truly was morning and that he actually was in his bedroom. The realness of the dream amazed Joe as he sat on the edge of the bed and collected his senses. He had the sensation that he had actually been in the dream. The feeling that only a few seconds before he had been somewhere other than his bed.

Do people have dreams like this? Why did this happen? Is this some kind of out of body experience? Should I tell anyone?

These were just some of the questions that he considered. Then he closed his eyes and retraced the dream to be sure not to forget any part of it. He didn't understand what had happened to him or why it happened but he was sure he had just experienced something special, and he didn't want to forget anything.

Although he didn't feel like he had just awoke from a good sleep, he still felt refreshed and vibrant, but there was an odd feeling too. Like something was missing or not finished yet. As he strained his thoughts of what it might be, it came to him. It hit him so hard, he wondered for a second if he was still dreaming. In a way he wished he had been. He formed the question that he suddenly realized needed answering.

Why didn't Lazarus go with Jesus and the disciples? Why wasn't he one to begin with? Wasn't he a close friend to Jesus? I think it says Jesus knew him and his sisters well. He was friends with them. If he was so close to Jesus, why was he not a disciple? This question pressed on Joe's mind as he reached for the

Bible on the nightstand. As he flipped through the Bible, he thought, *man, ain't I really worthy? Just witnessed the Bible first-hand and I don't even know where to find the story in the Bible.*

He placed the Bible back and ran his hand through his hair as if to wipe away some of the guilt. *I have to read more. I want to read more.* Joe reached for the Bible again but reality set in. He had to get ready for work. Reluctantly, Joe got to his feet as scenes of the dream ran through his mind again.

As the hot shower hit him in the face, with eyes closed, it hit him. The revelation to his question about Lazarus. Joe's eyes opened and water stung them. He turned around, wiped the water from his face, brushed his hair back and smiled an acknowledging smile. Immediately a peace fell over him. He knew without a doubt he had the answer he was supposed to have. The answer as to why Lazarus wasn't with Jesus or followed him after his raising.

Even though he was Jesus' close friend, Lazarus wasn't called to be a disciple. We're not all called to do the same job or same type of job. Perhaps we ALL have a unique calling.

He thinks he had heard this before. A preacher might have said it. *That we all are called according to His will.*

Maybe Lazarus wasn't supposed to be a disciple. What if his purpose, his empty hole to fill, his core purpose, was to be Jesus' friend and even die as part of his purpose for being? Had anyone realized this before about this story, Joe thought. *His main purpose in life might have been to simply die so Jesus could show the people that He can do all, including rising from the dead.* Joe stood motionless and let the thoughts sink in more. *What does this mean for me? It's a simple revelation but it means so much.*

What does this mean for me, Joe thought out loud.

"What?" Said Joe's wife.

"Huh?" Joe had not heard her enter the bathroom.

"You said what does something mean".

Despite being caught talking to himself, Joe smiled. Joe was happy. *Yeah,* he thought. *I feel different.* Maybe he had started filling his void, Joe thought.

* * * * *

The workday came and went. Mainly the usual stuff except for all the thoughts of Lazarus' story bouncing around his head all day. A co-worker remarked that something seemed different about Joe.

His purpose was simply to be there for Jesus; be His friend. That was his purpose. How awesome, Joe thought all day. *I want to find **my** purpose. What **is** mine?* Joe questioned, but unlike before, unlike while at the lake Saturday, this time the question burned in him a different way. Joe didn't feel depressed about it.

Wonder if it says anymore about the sisters? Wonder what their role was in God's plan? I have to read the Bible more. I want to read it more. The heck with watching the game tonight, Joe realized. *What is a game when I'm on the verge of figuring a few things out? I want to read. I want to know my purpose. So I can fill that hole; my abyss, and be happy again.*

If Joe only knew the journey that still awaited him....

CHAPTER 3

JESSE

Joe figured it was a good thing that he didn't want to see the game anyway. He did want to read but any other Monday this time of year, he would have been raising cane for being at the mall on a Monday night. He fussed at his wife for springing this trip on him after supper. The little one needed supplies for a school project and while they were near the mall, they may as well exchange her new cheerleading shoes that were the wrong size. He realized it was logical to take care of these things in one trip but it didn't make him any less agitated about it.

He sat on a bench outside the shoe store nodding off, waking up, looking around and then playing it off as if no one had seen. The night of dreaming may have taken more out of him than he realized. He was tired.

The mall wasn't crowded so it was easy for the man to notice Joe sitting there, fighting sleep like a toddler not wanting to take a nap.

"Mind if I sit here?"

Joe didn't mind but it did seem odd since there were plenty of seats around.

"Waiting on your wife?" The old man asked as he set down.

"Uh, yeah". Joe answered, as if not wanting to be bothered. "Never fails, a woman can change your plans any time."

"He-he", the man chuckled. "Yep, nothing like waiting on a woman." They both laughed as thoughts of the country song with the same statement came to mind.

They made small talk and discussed trivial things, including the game that was about to start.

"Yeah, it will be half over by the time I get home", Joe grumbled. Perhaps the aggravation had overcome the desire to read or perhaps Joe was just tired.

"Oh, is that what gotcha all riled up? About your plans tonight? Ya wanted to watch that game did you?"

"No, not really, I guess." Joe's eyes seemed to stare blank as in deep thought for a minute. Then he glanced at the man closer. *Boy, I must be really tired. Had a night of intense dreams and didn't miss a detail.* Joe thought as rubbing his hand on his shirt sleeve in thought of the detail of last night's dream. *Now I've let a total stranger sit beside me without noticing anything about him.* Joe guessed the man must have been late seventies, at least, maybe more, but he didn't recall the old guy moving like an older person when he walked up. He had white hair, a long, ungroomed beard and wore an old ball cap and old wore out over-alls. *The kind grandpa used to wear*, Joe recounted. Perhaps it was the brief memory of his grandpa that moved him, but he felt compelled to talk more with the old man.

"So what were you going to do?" the stranger asked.

"Huh, about what?" Joe asked.

"Tonight, this evening?"

"Oh, oh, yeah. I.... Well...." stuttered Joe. The old man looked at Joe as if to raise one eyebrow and already know the answer to come. Joe continued, "You know, it really doesn't matter. All that matters is doing what I'm supposed to do. She needed school supplies and shoes... and it's just fine that it's a Monday night", Joe said in a relieving tone. Like he had just found out all is going to be okay. Kind of the way he felt this morning.

"Well, that's good", said the old man smiling. "You sound like you're a good daddy to those girls."

Joe enjoyed their conversation about various things until the old man said he better be going.

"Mall's closing soon. Gotta go," he said rising to his feet.

"Oh, what's your name? I'm Joe". Joe extended his hand for a handshake. The old man reached for Joe's hand and said, "People just call me Jesse", and the man smiled and turned to walk away.

Later, as Joe lay in bed thinking about the encounter with the grandpa-figure type, he recounted some of the things Mr. Jesse had told him. Joe's new found friend reminded him that the 'Good Book' says to be a cheerful giver and always present yourself as such - cheerful, regardless of the situation, trouble, or trial. Just then Joe remembered a verse the old man gave him. He grabbed the Bible from the nightstand, turned on the lamp and flipped immediately to Jeremiah 29:11. *Was this correct? Was this what the old man told me to trust in?*

> 11 For I know the thoughts that I think toward
> you, saith the LORD, thoughts of peace,
> and not of evil, to give you an expected
> end.
> 12 Then shall ye call upon me, and ye shall
> go and pray unto me, and I will hearken
> unto you.
> 13 And ye shall seek me, and find me, when
> ye shall search for me with all your heart.

Joe pondered the meaning while the night remained silent. He was so intrigued with the versus that he wanted to know more. He wondered if there was another translation of the Bible in the house. Without wasting time to look, he grabbed his laptop and accessed the internet. Finally he found it.

> 11 'For I know the plans that I have for you,'
> declares the LORD, 'plans for welfare and
> not for calamity to give you a future and
> a hope.
> 12 'Then you will call upon Me and come and
> pray to Me, and I will listen to you.
> 13 'You will seek Me and find Me when you
> search for Me with all your heart.

I have a plan for you ran through Joe's mind. He repeated it to himself as he realized how amazing that this verse ties in so much with his quest for discovering his purpose. *Man, that dream last night was something else, and now this old man.*

"What are you doing?" Joe's wife asked, a bit annoyed about being woken up. It was 2am.

"Sorry, just looking up the verse that old man in the mall gave me tonight".

"Who?" She said.

"The old man I talked to while you were in the shoe store". Joe stated.

With eyes still closed and head buried in the pillow, she quietly chuckled and said, "You didn't look like you were talking to anyone to me. You were asleep when we came out of the store."

CHAPTER 4

TOUGH DAY

The puzzlement of the dreams was on Joe's mind when he awoke in the morning. His mall friend seemed even more perplexing than the Lazarus dream. The realness of both episodes is what pressed on Joe's mind the most. *How can this be so real?* Joe thought. Regardless of the oddity of the past couple of days, Joe was just glad it was all somehow providing some sort of relief from his unhappiness; his despair; his abyss.

And just who was this Jesse person? Joe questioned himself. *Was it a dream? If not, I wonder if he is some sort of preacher or something. He made me feel like I was around someone special. Had I fallen back asleep just before they came out?* Joe couldn't figure it out. Though he didn't know the answer, he was amazed that it didn't really matter that much. The relief he was feeling out-weighed the questions and that mattered the most to him he concluded.

Maybe I should tell her, Joe thought a few seconds later as he was in the shower. He questioned if it was right or not for him to keep this from his wife. He wasn't sure what 'this' actually meant though. *What would she think anyway? It's not like it would make a lot of sense to her. She knows I've not been the same the past year or so, but would all of this make sense?.*

Things had not been right for their marriage either. The arguments had seemed to taper off or at least been less intense as the distance between them had grown. Daily life though, appeared fairly normal and perhaps they both assumed that the problems were typical for people at this point of marriage, although he knew that summation was false.

Joe reveled in the revelations he had been given, but the avenue for the new-found inspiration weighed on his mind. Regardless, he had found himself kneeling to pray when he got up, even without realizing it. He thought about the ease of altering his habits, the revelations and the dreams on his way to work. Normally, it was a dash to the shower to make up for one or two snooze buttons he always found so easily. Joe hoped that his revelations, his new found desires: to read, to pray, would catapult him to a life of contentment and satisfaction and most of all, purpose. He assumed he was on the right path to closing his abyss. He thought, perhaps he never did really understand why or even when he had become so miserable and unstable. Even more, he wondered if he was really that different from most everyone else; just trudging through life and needing to suck it up and be tougher. What he did know for sure, at this point, was that these odd, unbelievable dreams were starting to relieve his pain. The pain that he blamed on that terrible empty feeling that had led him to depression.

If not depression, then some other awful, horrible mental and physiological state, Joe admitted to himself. A state he had to move away from or....

Joe wasn't sure what the 'or' actually might be but he was sure that his emptiness was leading to something. Something bad. And as much as he had wanted to escape, it had not dawned on him once, whether at church or in his sporadic, half-hearted, elementary attempts at prayer, that the answer might be found in the Bible, or even more puzzling, straight from God.

In the form of dreams? He asked himself.

Today, he was sure that things seemed to be pointing toward a path of recovery. A path away from misery and disappointment and toward a purpose-filled life. *Lazarus had purpose; the Bible says God has a plan for me, and I believe it.* Questions flashed in and out of his thoughts. Questions like, "who is Jesse?", "why these dreams?", but also more concrete and seemingly more sensible ones, like, "is all this from God or am I really so messed up that now I'm doubting my own sanity. The thought of it all not being from God disappointed Joe. He drove the next few miles without any thoughts, and then decided his sanity wasn't in question.

There's no way I'm 'losing it'. I feel too reassured that all will be okay.

Joe shrugged his shoulders, and smiled a half smile as he pulled into his parking space at work.

Joe would realize later that days like he is about to experience will become easier to overcome as he grows closer to God through his journey.

* * * * * *

"What the hell is this?" Joe didn't even have time to look up before a paper was shoved down on his desk. His boss must have darted through the open doorway so fast that the sound hadn't registered with him before the report came thundering down on his desk.

"They're returning the last two shipments. Last week's shipment was so bad that they don't want to even consider opening this one.... And it's our problem to get it back to us.... JOE, this is ridiculous." The boss stood in front of Joe's desk and just shook his head. Joe knew his boss was all business but even this type of behavior was out of character for him. Joe had seen him angry before but never to this degree.

Not like this. Not this much. Joe thought.

Joe scanned the paper to find the shipment amounts. "They both should fit on one truckload, so we can prevent two LTL charges", Joe said.

"Yeah. I know", said the boss, a little calmer but in a disappointed tone. "It's just that I thought you had this problem fixed. We can't keep going this way."

"I thought we did", responded Joe. "I at least thought we were past problems requiring full returns.... You know, it's like I told you; we are making progress. They said they would work with us as we put permanent fixes in place." Joe paused.

"They're not even going to open the newest shipment?" Joe asked. "They couldn't have received it until yesterday, so there's no way..."

"IT'S NOT OUR CUSTOMERS' responsibility to remove our defects from their shipments." Yelled Joe's boss. "Would YOU?. If you were them?"

The only sensible, responsible answer was "No", Joe said slowly shaking his head with his teeth clinched together and lips protruding out. The boss left the room.

The only right answer is the one he already knows, Joe yelled to himself about his boss. *They just told us Thursday that they would work through this with us. He knows that. He heard the conference call. He hadn't done anything to fix this... he hardly even spoke up during the hour-long conference call... and now he wants to act like he didn't hear it. Guess I get to be the fall guy for this.* For weeks, it had seemed to Joe that office politics were singling him out as the one to take the blame for recent issues with production.

Joe put his head in his hands before heading out to the shop floor. He thought how terrible it would be to lose his job. *Hardly have any equity in the house... selling in this market... yeah, right.... The car payments; I can't trade her car... hmm, yeah... end up having to let my truck go... she wouldn't stand for losing hers.* On and on the thoughts came. They seemed to sing a chorus of despair to aid in his demise.

Finally, he shook his head and tried to focus. He had to get on top of the quality problem. "It's obvious he's sticking me out on my own limb about this", Joe thought out loud as he walked toward the office door.

By mid-morning, things had not gotten better. It seemed to Joe that everything that could go wrong was happening. On top of everything at work, his wife had called and a simple question had turned into an argument. Joe tried to remain strong but it was shaping up to be a really hard day; machines broke, production started falling behind, the maintenance supervisor called in sick, and now marriage friction decided to jump into the middle of it. Joe tried to stay calm but the pressure was mounting. He felt anxiety building. He felt the pressures of the day marching toward a bigger problem. One that overwhelmingly dwarfed everything else. A problem that felt like a full solar eclipse was setting in to block out any ray of light that may had been present just a few hours before.

The blackout Joe felt was the re-opening of the abyss. As hard as he tried to ignore it, he couldn't. The next few minutes seemed like hours, as Joe now stood frozen. Eyes fixed straight ahead but seeing nothing. Which is how he began to feel inside; nothing; empty. Simultaneous thoughts pounded at his demeanor: Work strains, marriage strains, concerns, worries, anxiety....

I can't lose this job... this job market is terrible.

If we had to move... we can' t move. The kids are so rooted in their schools....

She wouldn' t want to anyway... that could be the final straw for us....

I should have been saving more money... if we hadn't got that new SUV....

That boss... he knows... this is no one's fault... we just have to work through it....

The serenade of pleasant thoughts he had experienced earlier in the morning were long forgotten now.

"The abyss is coming back", Joe mouthed to himself. The sound of production machines seemed to hum in unison and drown out any chance to catch his spiraling demise as he stood motionless, letting all the negativity soak in. Emotions now switched to hopeless feelings of inadequacy. During the past year, the abyss had been carved out with feelings of worthlessness, shame, and guilt. His thoughts proclaimed it repeatedly until he accepted defeat. The path to recovery he had stepped onto just a few hours before was turning out to be a twisted, sick, cruel joke; setting him up to feel happy and hopeful, but ending in a sudden fall to utter disappointment. Like a lone miner unknowingly digging for fools gold, he had furtively fallen back into a pit of despair. Darts of anger shot through him as realization of deceit set in.

After a promising start to his day, and much more critical, a promising step in his journey, Joe was letting the abyss back into his life.

Just as fast as it did at the lake Saturday, it's happening again, Joe realized. Except this time, it's worse. At this moment, Joe started to angrily question the past few nights; *the revelations, the dreams, Jesse....* He shook his head in disappointment but also to try and overcome sudden thoughts of dis-belief.

Yet somehow, just like scattered times before, and perhaps from lack of alternatives, he decided to press on. Still standing motionless he weighed the alternating thoughts; believe that he does have hope at a purpose-filled, happy life or relegate himself to simply surviving. After several more minutes, which seemed like hours, Joe took a deep breath and squared his shoulders and thought, *ok, that's enough. Suck it up Joe.* He put his hands on his hips, breathed in deep, and exhaled slowly. Like a boxer standing for the final round, he readied himself for more abuse. He decided to dig deep and find the stubborn determination that had always carried him through. Right through to the point he is now; just pressing on.

Pain and emptiness is just the way life is, Joe concluded. He heard the machines; a phone ringing; a door closing down the hall and he quickly continued his return to consciousness. He put a smile on his face. Not a happy smile; just one that would hopefully help mask his inner unstableness and help carry him through the rest of the day. *Just accept it. That's just the way life is. Accept it,* he thought, and turned to leave his office and get back to work.

* * * * * *

The aroma of dinner cooking greeted Joe when he came through the front door. The ride home from work had been quite and complacent, like a sports team returning home after a hard-fought loss. No one saying a word, but silently reassuring themselves that they had given their all. Like an underdog team marching thru the playoffs, only to come up short in the state title. Sadness and heartbreak accompanied with surreal contentment and comfort for putting up a good fight. This is how Joe felt after his challenging day. Except, instead of a life lesson learned from a sporting event, this day was a vicious reminder of real life. Settling for a moral victory by simply surviving the day's contest was not much consolation for Joe, and he knew it. He was tired of settling in life. He had worn the plastic smile to weather the onslaught of challenges until he finally found a stopping point to head home.

The day had already begun turning dark when he had made it to his car. He had ridden home in silence, without the radio and without much thought. Mental fatigue had been a gracious gift that prevented more analysis of his experiences the previous 12 hours. Joe knew that if he had dwelt on the emptiness of the day, it could have allowed the abyss to enlarge even more.

This morning he had been sure that it was starting to shrink; that somehow, even he, in his futile attempts at Christian living had stumbled into a path of recovery that revolved around some God-given dreams, and a new-found desire to read the Bible. Now he wasn't so sure about the dreams and he was even more unsure about the internal pep-talk he had given himself before lunch. It had managed to only keep the abyss in-check; not relieve it.

Am I really supposed to just suck it up and find a way to simply get by? Is that all life is... just suffer through it? Joe had shaken his head each time these thoughts darted into his mind. He was sure that this was not how life is supposed to be, and thankfully, finding the answers to his life questions was closer than he realized. Nighttime was coming and he was only a few hours away from another step on his journey.

Spaghetti sauce, Joe whined as he made his entrance. The smell of her spaghetti sauce greeted Joe at the door. Onions, peppers, tomato sauce and garlic drowned his sense of smell. As tired as he was, it didn't really matter to him that his least favorite meal was for dinner. He was just relieved to be home.

"WHAT?", she asked, peering from the kitchen.

Joe tried to quickly turn his head to hide the expression he must have made when the garlic smacked him in the face. "Huh?", Joe asked while removing his jacket.

"You don't want this do you?", she fired back.

Boy, I must've really told on myself without even knowing it, he thought. "Wh..., uh..., OH, spaghetti?!", he said, trying to act like he was surveying the kitchen to discover what was for dinner.

"Yeah, right", she responded dejectedly and sarcastically, returning to her culinary duties.

How many times have I told her that I'm just not a fan of spaghetti.... After the day I had.... She wants to start in on me.... I swear.... I ought to....

"Hey dad... will you help me with this?", his oldest daughter asked, breaking the tirade of his thoughts. As he stepped toward her, he remembered his wife's call from earlier in the day. *Oh crap... the argument this morning... should've made time to call her back.... That's why she's ill at me.*

Bending to a knee beside his daughter at the kitchen table, he hugged her with one arm and answered, "'Course I will honey", and helped her with homework.

Despite the tension from the start of the evening, Joe managed to not make things worse and thanked his wife for dinner. That smoothed things a bit more and they both seemed a little relieved. After helping put away dishes, Joe retired to the spare bedroom where he sometimes read. Instead of grabbing the day's newspaper or a magazine, he stopped by the bedroom nightstand to retrieve the Bible. Despite the troubling day and exhaustion, he still had a smoldering ember of desire to read. Admittedly, a far less intense flame than present last night and much less than after seeing the Lazarus story the night before, but regardless, he found himself walking down the hall to a place of solitude to read the Word.

Where do I start, rang in his ears as he sat in the chair in the corner, looking down at the closed Bible like a hungry, humble, quite child, waiting to be fed. Joe stared intently at the cover, as if waiting for it to open. The usual sounds of the house carried down the hall. The youngest being told to get a bath before it gets too late; the oldest heading upstairs to her seclusion for the evening; the faint sound of a TV playing in the den. Joe sat motionless and without thought for a long time. Perhaps sitting down without any distractions was a welcomed relief. He sat perfectly still and enjoyed the solitude.

Finally, Joe broke the stalemate and reached to open It. As he did, he felt like a child cautiously opening a fragile gift, not knowing exactly where to start or how to do go about it. Suddenly he heard footsteps coming down the hall. His motions froze and he contemplated setting the Gift on the desk beside him to prevent being questioned.

"What'cha doing?", his wife asked, stopping at the doorway.

"Just reading", was his answer, with both forearms laying on top of the Book.

"Oh", she said, and moved on down the hall.

If she realizes I'm taking time to read the Bible, she might ask more..., Joe thought questioningly. *It's just... I'm not sure what I would tell her. How would I tell her about these... dreams, encounters....* Joe continued to reflect, his elbow now propped up on the arm of the chair and his forehead resting in his palm.

Man, I'm tired, he realized. *Maybe tomorrow night would be better.* The thought didn't soothe his exhaustion and he picked his head up.

Joe continued to sit motionless and began trying to recall different points in his life to determine when he last read the Bible on his own. Of course he read along *at church*, he thought. Then, as though he was speaking convincingly into the empty room in front of him, he thought, *we've occasionally been involved with a series at church*, he recounted. Then with disappointment and a gentle shake of his head, he couldn't recall what they were about. He pushed back deeper in the chair and continued to ponder.

There was that time we helped with youth group.... I even taught the lesson that day.... John, yeah..., I think we taught from John, he said convincingly to himself.

After possibly several more minutes of random recounts, Joe breathed in deep and emotionally felt the pain of his abyss as he inhaled long and slow. His legs jerked slightly as if nervously attempting to avoid the unwanted return. The twitch caused the Bible to slide off his lap to the edge of the chair and then to the floor, despite his attempt to catch it before It landed. As he leaned over to retrieve it, he realized how sleepy he was.

Must be from sitting here so long, he concluded as he yawned wide and long. He sat upright on the edge of the chair with the Bible in hand. His eyes were so drowsy that they closed as he yawned again. Like a student caught sleeping in class, he popped them right back open. An odd thought filled his mind....

Am I asleep?

He quickly leaned up more and despite thoughts of foolishness flashing in his mind, he spun his head around fast to see if he was still asleep in the chair. His heart rate jumped. Still twisted around looking behind him at the chair, he sat motionless for a few quick breaths.

The sounds from the evening's tasks were diminishing as everyone had retreated to their rooms. His heart raced in his ears and the solitude of the stillness added to his hysteria. He blinked several times and gently leaned forward, as if peaking over his shoulder. His vision was blurry. He blinked more and considered jumping to his feet in fear as he began to focus more clearly.

He wasn't sure what he wanted to see. A quick remembrance of Lazarus replaced his anxiety and fear with excitement. Still trying to focus better, and without moving more, he began cutting his eyes from right to left and back again. He did it several times. His heart pounded so hard that it scared him while he tried to determine if he was asleep.

AM I???? He thought.

Could I be.... flashed in his thoughts.

He was still twisted in an awkward position with his right hand on the left arm of the chair as he considered what to do next. Then he squeezed the chair with his hand.

I feel it, he said to himself as he squeezed it. *Details! Not in a dream... not to this degree*, he thought. *But, the robe... I felt the robe, and the sand. It sifted through my fingers.*

He sniffed. He blinked. Like a detective looking for the final big clue to solve the case, Joe sought his answer to whether or not he was dreaming. Or in some sort of trance.

Thinking about a dream while dreaming... no way.... Is it possible? He asked himself with excitement.

"Dad."

Joe uncoiled from his twisted position quickly and faced the doorway opening while trying to grab a touch of reality. He tried to erase the bewilderment that he knew his face displayed. He started to answer but the confusion that was still present prevented him from forming any words. It felt like minutes passed before she spoke again.

"Goodnight," the young voice said.

With a relieving exhale, he finally smiled and responded, "uh, 'night dear."

As quickly as she had appeared in the doorway, she was gone again; off to bed.

He still felt his face blushing and he chuckled at the thoughts that had been coursing through his mind.

Dreaming, in a dream, while thinking about a dream. He laughed to himself and shook his head.

The chair welcomed him as he scooted back into it, still searching for a full dose of reality. As full consciousness set in, he decided to not think about the wild thoughts he had just seconds before, hopefully erasing the embarrassment that still showed on his face.

Like a captain righting a ship, Joe regained the purpose of his solitude time and opened the Bible lying in his lap. He wanted to read. He wanted relief. He wanted to find answers. He subconsciously wanted to step back onto the recovery path that he had found this morning. The pains of his day along with the agony of his abyss reminded him why he wanted to read. He wanted to regain control of the abyss. Most of all he wanted to find his purpose, like his revelation about Lazarus, and without completely realizing it at the time, he wanted to get closer to God.

Joe was glad that the desire to read and the reasons why had quickly returned.

He quickly thumbed through the Bible and randomly stopped at John chapter 11. As soon as he began to read, thoughts and questions jumped from the page. He wasn't surprised that he happened to land at this story. Beginning with the first verse, he was amazed at the readability and the excitement he felt.... *Mary and her sister Martha*, Joe said raising his thoughts in excitement. *The sisters.*

> 1 Now a certain man was sick, Lazarus of Bethany, the village of Mary and her sister Martha.
>
> 2 It was the Mary who anointed the Lord with ointment, and wiped His feet with her hair, whose brother Lazarus was sick.
>
> 3 So the sisters sent word to Him, saying, "Lord, behold, he whom You love is sick".

He couldn't help but acknowledge the mental pictures from his dream. He could see their sadness and puffy, swollen, tear-filled eyes. He closed his eyes and reflected on the dream. Without fore-thought, he uttered, "Thank you Lord". Suddenly the Lazarus dream somehow became even more real. *Thank you, Lord*, he thought again, *for letting me dream this.* The Bible and the dream intertwined perfectly. Joe almost felt euphoric as he continued.

At verse 3 he remembered them asking Jesus about coming to help. "Why didn't you come when they told you?", he could hear them asking. He continued to reflect on the dream.

4 But when Jesus heard this, He said, "This
   sickness is not to end in death, but for the
   glory of God, so that the Son of God may
   be glorified by it."

At verse 5, he remembered the smile and reassuring nod
that Jesus gave as he turned to walk away after the reunion of
Lazarus with his family.

5 Now Jesus loved Martha, and her sister,
   and Lazarus. Thoughts poured out of
   his mind as he continued. *He* was *a close
   friend to Jesus.... Lazarus must have known
   a lot about Jesus.... Wow.... I never thought
   about Him having earthly 'friends'.* Joe read
   in amazement and awe at the realness of
   the story. *Why had this never been so real
   when I heard it in the past?*

As an interruption to his barrage of scripture-induced
thoughts, Joe considered if perhaps it was because he had
never wanted it to be real. Quickly, the excitement of his
reading outweighed the dart of guilt posed by his question.

*They were close friends.... Wonder if they confided in each
other.... What did Lazarus do for a living? Carpentry? Did they
ever work together?* These were some of the many thoughts

Joe had. Like turning on a floodlight, Joe quickly processed the realization that Jesus had a real life; that the Bible is only excerpts. If not for passion to keep reading, he may had sat and pondered on the realization longer, but he yearned to read more....

6 So when He heard that he was sick, He then stayed two days longer in the place where He was.

7 Then after this He said to the disciples, "Let us go to Judea again."

8 The disciples said to Him, "Rabbi, the Jews were just now seeking to stone You, and are You going there again?"

9 Jesus answered, "Are there not twelve hours in the day? If anyone walks in the day, he does not stumble, because he sees the light of this world.

10 "But if anyone walks in the night, he stumbles, because the light is not in him."

11 This He said, and after that He said to them, "Our friend Lazarus has fallen asleep; but I go, so that I may awaken him out of sleep."

12 The disciples then said to Him, "Lord, if he has fallen asleep, he will recover."

> 13 Now Jesus had spoken of his death, but
> they thought that He was speaking of
> literal sleep.
> 14 So Jesus then said to them plainly, "Lazarus
> is dead,

At verse 14, he thought, *man, didn't they get it?* He read on....

> 15 and I am glad for your sakes that I was not
> there, so that you may believe; but let us
> go to him."
> 16 Therefore Thomas…

"Thomas!" Joe said excitedly, remembering his question from his dream. Like a kid pouncing on Christmas morning presents, Joe read the rest of verse 16.

> Who is called Didymus, said to his fellow
> disciples, "Let us also go, so that we may
> die with Him."

"That we may die with him", he read out loud. He read it again to himself several times like a sponge soaking up juices. *Wow... willing to die with him... and they call him a doubter.... Doubter? That's not right! Or wait, did he say that out of spight?* He didn't care to have the perfect answer. Having the questions seemed to intrigue him more.

Flashes of Jesus' miracles and the simple nod and smile exploded in Joe's mind. The love he felt during his dream; the peace and contentment he felt. It all flooded Joe and he began to cry. As he sought to control his sobs, he gently wiped away tears, one eye at a time. *Thank you Lord for blessing me.... Thank you Jesus for loving me....* Over and over, Joe cried this prayer while peace and assuredness enveloped him.

Finally, minutes later, Joe continued reading. Then he paused and looked up. The house remained perfectly still and silent. The only sound interrupting the quietness was the refrigerator's ice maker dumping another batch of ice. *She must have gone on to bed,* he thought regarding his wife. Then he thought about the time. *Got to be getting late.*

Before he would let his devout attention slip, he looked right back down at the Word. He finished chapter 11 with many more thoughts, revelations and questions than he would remember tomorrow. He flipped back to chapter 6 and read about the feeding of the 5000. It seemed every verse produced thoughts. He wondered how the seemingly simple children's story could actually be so intriguing and thought provoking.

1 After these things Jesus went away to
   the other side of the Sea of Galilee (or
   Tiberias)

2 A large crowd followed Him, because they
saw signs which He was performing on
those who were sick.

At verse 2 he thought about the miracles and how he wished it went on to tell about them. His mind raced so fast from one thought to another that he actually felt exhausted when he did slow down to catch his breath.

All the miracles and some still wanted to kill Him, he thought. *So many people healed and cured and cleansed... and the Jews... the Romans....* Before he could trip into feeling angry about them, the love aspect of Jesus engulfed him. *I've never really grasp it.* He shook his head in astonishment that possibly this; what he was reading, is what Christianity is about. About Christ, about love, about peace, about assuredness; not about... church stuff.... Joe was processing more channels of thought than he could maintain. He wanted to focus on the contemplation that there seemed to be a huge difference between 'church and religion' and what he was reading, while at the same time, he wanted to process deeper, the mental image of the scriptures. Along with those paths, he pondered their meanings to his life. The waves of thoughts continued while he continued reading.

John 6, verse 9; "There is a lad here who has five barley loaves and two fish, but what are these for so many people?"

Being enthralled with his read, Joe's mind race with darts of questions.

Why was the boy there? Where did he come from? Was he with his parents? Was that his lunch? Did the rest of the crowd not bring one? Did he want to feed Jesus and the disciples?

10 Jesus said, "Have the people sit down." Now there was much grass in the place. So the men sat down, in number about five thousand.
11 Jesus then took the loaves, and having given thanks, He distributed to those who were seated; likewise also of the fish as much as they wanted.

Five thousand? That must have taken a long time for that many to eat. As much as they wanted? Man, that was a heck of a buffet. Joe chuckled at his thought.

He continued to read.

12 When they were filled, He said to His disciples, "Gather up the leftover fragments so that nothing will be lost."

Finally, he thought about quitting for the night or at least finding out the time. He looked around the room for a clock, then went right back to reading. He read about the disciples sailing away after Jesus fed the 5000 and thought it sounded strange.

> 17 and after getting into a boat, they started to cross the sea to Capernaum. It had already become dark, and Jesus had not yet come to them.
>
> 18 The sea began to be stirred up because a strong wind was blowing.

He kept reading, then pausing to reflect and absorb the versus. He could not believe all the thoughts and questions that came to mind.

Somewhere around verse 25 he fell asleep.

CHAPTER 5

PEARLY WHITES

Joe's chin was nearly touching his chest as his snoring grew louder. The Bible had slid off his lap and nestled between his left thigh and the arm of the chair. The house was still void of sound and the slightest movement would have produced a thundering noise. Joe's head falling deeper into his lap caused him to wake with a gasp for breath. If not for the intense heartburn, it may have taken him longer to fully awaken and survey his surroundings.

Oh... that spaghetti sauce, he thought, putting his hand on his chest. He winced and sighed before deciding to stand up. He made sure the Bible was closed neatly without any wrinkled or folded pages as he moved to the edge of the chair.

He found himself standing in the kitchen without clearly realizing he had walked into it. He felt awake due to the intense heartburn but still groggy from being suddenly awaken. After taking an indigestion pill and drinking a glass of water, he decided he was now too awake to go straight to bed, so he headed toward the den.

Need to let this pill take affect first anyway, he thought, grabbing at the front of his shirt again. *I never changed out of my work clothes*, came to mind as he thought about all the reading he had done.

He made his way to the sofa in the den and instinctively reached for the remote control as he eased into his second bed of the night. To be sure and not wake the family, he was pressing the volume down button as he turned on the TV. Once reaching a soft level, he began pressing the channel up button. Without giving the scene time to register in his mind, he began channel surfing. As he pressed, he thought, *maybe I'll watch some of that Christian TV.* Before he got there though, he found something else.

OH, I LOVE THIS MOVIE, immediately registered with him and he stopped pressing buttons, bumped the volume up a notch and laid the remote beside him on the couch.

"MOVE, move son!", came from the TV. Scenes of football players practicing filled the screen.

"YOU GOTTA GO; you gotta go now...."

"Ya godda want it...."

"OH YEAH, ya got to want it!", came from one of Joe's favorite actors.

As Joe entranced into the movie he had seen several times, he remembered that it's a true story.

Man, what a great story.... What a time in history.... Such an amazing, touching story.

Sounds of a coach's whistle stops the practice on the screen and Joe re-directs his attention from his historical reflectance. A whistle clinched firmly between the pearly white teeth of Denzel Washington is the origin of the sound. *They couldn't have gotten a better person to play the role*, Joe thinks.

"'Remember The Titans' will continue", interrupts Joe's thoughts as the movie goes to commercial.

Then for some reason, the challenges of Joe's day at work revived and he leaned his head back on the couch. After exhaling and realizing the pill had worked, he considers going to bed. *I got to sleep.... Man, I don't want to be tired tomorrow.*

Why do I bother, comes to mind as he thinks about the headaches and stress of his job. *I have to have income but man.... I'm not trying to start a pity party but why do these thoughts pop up now?*

Talking about having a meaning in life.... What about that coach? The struggles; the challenges.... Now that's worth working for. Joe thinks about the basis of the movie: integration, racial tension, etc. *This coach had to break down barriers, inspire young men to work and play together, unite a community.... Man, what a calling.* Then, surprisingly, like being nudged from behind unexpectedly, Joe remembered the reason for his abyss.

Calling, purpose, reason for living, fulfillment.... Except Joe wasn't quite as timid about his abyss. He hoped that his encounter with the Bible had closed it back up a little. He still had his head reclined and his eyes pointed at the ceiling while he thought.

Of all the people I know... day in... day out... all the people at work... church... friends... heck, everybody.... Have they found their purpose? Do I really think my answer to find relief, to find happiness, is to find my purpose... and there'll actually be an answer?

It sounded like the front door slamming as Joe corrected himself. He paused for a second to strain his ears to see if a door really had shut before completing his thought. *Jeremiah 29:11. Ok, Lord, I believe.*

Scenes of the movie flashed in his mind as he continued realizing that the coach must have surely known his calling. Joe raised his head to think deeper. *What an awesome work to do... what that coach did.* As scenes continued to scroll, Joe became emotional as he reflected on his reading earlier and on his dreams and on the now apparent realization that he does have a deeper meaning for his life; a purpose. *One that will fulfill me*, he thought. *God does want to bless me... with a fulfilled life*. He thanked God again while he prayed.

Joe wiped tears from his cheeks, then sniffed, and looked at the clock on the microwave in the kitchen, which he could see through the opening above the bar. Squinting his eyes didn't help determine the time, and he realized tears were puddled between his eyelids. He ran his finger through the creases in his closed eyes to remove them, blinked a few times and looked again. It was 2:07. He decided to go to bed.

* * * * * *

Why is my arm getting wet? Feels like water splashing on it? Joe asked himself. He tossed and turned and tried to fall asleep. *I can't get to sleep if the bed doesn't stop swaying like this.* After a few more seconds, he thought, m*y sleeve is going to be SOAKED.* Shaking his head in aggravation, he sarcastically continued, w*ell ain't this great*, as the bed continued to sway.

"ROW!" a voice shouted.

"FASTER!" yelled another.

"It's still there!"

"What is it?" another voice cried.

"JUST ROW!" The first voice repeated.

The sound of people shouting annoyed Joe even more. His sleeve was getting soaked and he couldn't get to sleep for all the ruckus. *I am so tired*, he whined.

"You MUST row!", Yelled the voice again. This time it sounded closer. Amongst the chorus of commands, Joe thought he recognized one of the voices.

"ROW" was shouted again and he was sure it was even closer. This time he was sure they had to be standing right beside his bed.

Bed? Joe thought.

Then he sat straight up and was nudged from behind. Fear and trepidation over took Joe. People all around him was beating the water profusely in vain attempts to make their oars work in unison. It was nighttime. The only light illuminating his surroundings was the futile attempt of the moon to shed light in between small openings in the clouds. The wind began to blow hard. The boat started rocking side to side. A storm was brewing. The clouds moved fast in front of the moon, teasing the water surface with glimpses of light. Joe could feel waves white-capping against the side of the boat. He was scared. With his head on a swivel, he spun frantically to try and make sense of it all.

Then he realized he had an oar in his hand. He looked down at it while the boat rocked back and forth. Sounds around him registered more clearly now. As he continued to comprehend his environment, he knew where he was, just not what he was; or what was happening. He sensed that the source of their fright was coming up from behind.

"It's getting closer", one shouted in fear.

"ROW", shouted the first voice.

What is getting closer, Joe thought, and he turned his head around quickly to look over his right shoulder. He was shocked to see how quickly his thoughts shifted from the subject of the dream to a startling, surprising twist. His first impulse was to laugh.

"Oh, dat's right! You gotta row."

"We got ta go! Ya godda row now JOE!"

Joe could not believe what he was seeing. Right there, inches behind him; just behind his right shoulder, he was there. Joe couldn't believe it, but it was him. With sounds of the helpless voyage all around, Joe stared right into the face of the familiar voice. With pearly white teeth glistening at him from a big smile, Joe couldn't help but feel the urge to laugh at the reality that right there in the middle of his dream, was Denzel Washington.

"Yuh gotta row. Oh yeah, that's rrrighttt", he said smiling.

"Ya godda row us away from here", smiling even bigger. "HE, HE", he chuckled, flashing his pearly whites.

"OH, that's right", nodding with exaggeration. "Ya gotta row the boat".

Joe tried to obey the order as he finally exploded with laughter. He laughed hysterically as he tried to get in timing with the rowing. *How crazy is this? I know I'm dreaming and I somehow invite my favorite actor into it.* Joe continued to laugh. *Oh, this is great!*

Before he could enjoy anymore of the dream, the frightened members of the boat got his attention.

"Dear God, help us", yelled one of them.

"This is what we get for leaving Rabbi behind", another said.

"If He were here, surely He would protect us from this apparition walking on the water toward us", the first voice cried.

Then the chorus of commands re-started as the boat's passenger's turned to face ahead and resume their plight.

"We're too far from shore... ROW", shouted a voice.

Suddenly, several of them stopped rowing and then others and Joe realized they were looking behind him. In bewildered relief, they all looked in the direction of the source of their fear. The boat had stopped swaying and quickly the water calmed and the clouds parted. The moon brightened the night and it became eerily silent. The storm was gone. Then Joe began to realize not only where he was but even better, where he was... in the Bible.

John, chapter 6, after He fed the 5000, he confirmed. His night's reading was fresh in his mind.

The boat gently leaned to the right causing a mild splash and then stabilized again. The splash was awkwardly calm compared to the violent waves that had battered the boat just a few seconds before. Euphoria and excitement immediately coursed through him. Joe knew that Jesus had stepped into the boat just a few feet behind him. Again, like at Lazarus' tomb, overwhelming euphoria and emotions swept over him like a wave. He fought to remain in control, though he realized how odd his desire was... *I'm dreaming.*

Regardless, this time Joe wanted to be sure to see Him and watch the final seconds of the dream with a sense of assuredness and confidence, grasping every detail he could muster. As he turned around, in what felt like slow motion, he hoped that he was prepared to see Him face-to-face. His heartbeat jumped so fast that later he thought he would have passed out if not for the thud at the front of the boat that shook the vessel and caused Joe to wabble and quickly look forward again. "HUHHH", Joe exclaimed as he turned his head back toward the front excitedly. The boat had unexpectedly reached the shore.

Joe wasn't sure when he actually returned to his bed. He was already deep in revelation about his 3D Bible encounter, thinking about verse 21, when the sound of his alarm clock alerted him that it was officially over.

John 6:21 So they were willing to receive Him into the boat, and immediately the boat was at the land to which they were going.

He had a sense of disappointment for not completing the turn that would have brought him face-to-face with Christ, but his new revelation was quickly erasing it. He hit the snooze button without moving anything but his arm. He didn't want to lose his train of thought.

If we let Christ in our life... if we let Him be part of our life... NO, if we let Christ lead us.... Yeah, that's it. Lead, not just be... part of it, or some minor, Sunday only thing, then... then everything will be better. We'll reach our destination, our calling, our purpose, our happiness, our contentment.

Joe grinned like he just won a prize and delighted himself in his discovery, then continued with his revelation. *Once He stepped into the boat, they reached the shore.* Joe laid motionless in admiration of the story and the revelations he received from it. He also reveled in the delight that he had been allowed to experience it first hand and his desire to read the Bible was overwhelming.

John, chapter 6... I want to read it again. He was experiencing a realization that the Bible was actually more profound and deeper than he had ever grasped or imagined. *I just read this chapter a few hours ago... I didn't catch this... it's like there's so much more than... like the lessons to be learned go further... like there's different levels of understanding or something... depending on what I'm ready to comprehend.... Like there's an endless supply of knowledge to be gained.*

He didn't understand why he was getting to experience it first-hand but he was thankful he was. He began thanking the Lord over and over. *Thank you God.... Thank you Lord, Thank you Jesus,* jumped from his lips and his thoughts as he lay there. Over and over he thanked Him. Before answering his need to get up, he remembered a point that his pastor had made the past Sunday; '*sometimes our biggest challenge; our point of most fear; the part where we have to hold on the greatest; is just before we reach our destination; our blessing*'. The connection to his dream, *just like the disciples in the boat,* caused him to grin again in admiration.

Joe prayed some more and then headed to the shower, shaking his head in amazement. He felt awe-struck and wondered in anticipation of just how much more life-changing revelations may be in store for him. Then he thanked God some more.

CHAPTER 6

ATTIC TREASURE

I need a study Bible, Joe decided as he stepped from the shower. *We had one... I think it's on the bookshelf in the spare bedroom.*

Clothed with only a towel, he headed down the hall, careful not to slip on the hardwood with his wet feet. Realizing the time, he stopped by the youngest one's bedroom to wake her for school.

"Hun, time to get up", he said, hiding his toweled body around the corner of the doorway, leaving only his head viewable from the room. As typical, there was no movement from beneath the bundle of sheet and comforter.

"Sweetheart, time to get up", he added.

This gentle command got the reaction he was expecting. The covers raised up, a groan came from beneath them, then a petite arm became visible as the covers were shoved downward just enough to expose a nest of beautiful auburn-red hair.

Joe smiled and chuckled and said, "Love you, hun", then decided he had better wake up the rest of the family. Before he retreated down the hall back to the bedroom, he heard his wife say, "I'm getting up", and not in a pleasant tone. Without offering up a sacrificial salutation, he decided just to continue on his hunt.

At the bookshelf, his right index finger traced along the rows of books as he scanned.

Not here.

With his left hand still clenching the towel closed around his waist, he stared blankly into the bookshelf. *Where could it be?*

Sounds of the household coming to life began echoing through the hall. His wife had made it into the kitchen. A cabinet door shut loudly, then the youngest one's bedroom door closed shut, assuring him that she too was awake and readying herself for the school day. The oldest one pounded down the stairs, yelled a hurried, unaffectionate "Bye", and was off to start the day.

Instead of giving up on finding the study guide, Joe returned to the bedroom to dress so he could search the attic before leaving for work. After dressing, he hurriedly rushed upstairs.

"This place is a mess", he said opening the door. The cool of the autumn morning caused him to shiver as he stepped into the uninsulated attic storage area. The small room was accessible through a doorway to the right of the stair landing. It was usually only entered when another collection of items were deemed worthy of adding to the clutter. Most additions to the stockpile were done without any forethought to organization resulting in random stacks of boxes intermingled with various other items collected over the years. Some boxes had not been opened since the last move the family made several years before. It was in these boxes, that Joe thought he would find the study guide.

The cardboard storage boxes and the tape holding them together showed signs of many years of aging. Years of hot and cold weather had caused the tape to discolor and become brittle. The sides of the boxes had begun loosing their integrity and were bulging out. Bedrails and two headboards leaned against the wall behind one stack of boxes. A computer monitor the size of an old television sat on top of a child-size pool table.

Man, forgot about that thing. We must have played hundreds of games....

The monitor had discolored as well. The top and corners had turned from cream color to a light brown. *Why do we keep this stuff?*

Joe stood just inside the entrance, observing all the family artifacts. He stepped over an old keyboard, careful not to let his socks snag on the rough texture of the pressboard flooring. He vaguely remembered packing up books and other office-type supplies when they moved last time, so he decided to start his search by opening boxes. He scanned the area one more time for a clue that may tip him where to find the treasure, then stepped again toward the nearest stack of boxes.

"Owe, dang it!" Though he knew to be cautious, it happened anyway.

Splinter, he said to himself, dancing on one foot, while steadying himself with one hand lying on top of the boxes. After his grimace dance, he performed a balancing act that a ballerina would admire and brought his left foot up, resting it on his right knee. With careful attention, he found the end of the toothpick-sized missile that pierced him. After removing it, he placed his foot back on the floor, shifted his weight around a few times and decided he must have gotten all of it. Holding the splinter between his thumb and finger in front of his face, he thought, *so much pain from something so small,* and tossed it aside.

With attention back on his objective, he cupped his right hand and slid his fingers under the top flap of the box in front of him. The tape had fully deteriorated, so he gently pulled up and opened what he thought was just a corrugated storage box. Instead, he quickly realized that what he had opened was a treasure box.

His expression sank with heartfelt sentiment. "Awe, man, look at this", he said quietly to himself as he pushed both flaps open. Immediately, a torrid mix of emotions swept over him, like a wave crashing to shore. The treasure chest before him contained keepsakes of days gone by. Family pictures, snapshots of vacations, elementary school photos, child artwork, and other memory-inducing artifacts thrust a lump the size of an apple in his throat. The children looking up at him had seemingly overnight turned into young adults and had long since abandoned the years stored away in this corner of the attic, as well as his memory.

Like an archaeologist uncovering rare fossils, he carefully sifted through the treasures, pausing as he unearthed each new find and letting the memories flood over him.

Vacation. She was only five or six, I think. The framed snapshot he held contained an image he had long forgotten. Holding the chunk of gold with both hands, he gazed into it and the memories poured in.

Sounds of the beach carried him away. The ocean crashed against the sand. Seagulls flew overhead, cawing as they went by. The sun beat down on them relentlessly. Sounds of a sunny summer day at the beach were all around; children playing, music from a nearby radio, people laughing. Water splashed as waves broke near the shore, washed up, and then receded. Sand clung to his legs and arms as he rested himself next to the sandcastle they were engineering. In the foreground, the oldest child stood smiling for the camera like only an innocent five year old can; not a care or worry in the world. Behind her was Joe, the lead architect busying himself with the task at hand. Then a few feet beyond the sandcastle was the little one, just old enough to sit upright, enjoying a pacifier, securely shaded from the July sun by a beach umbrella. Joe's wife, standing with her back to the water and feet in the edge of the surf, had snapped the simple picture, that now seemed heir-loom worthy.

Suddenly a large drop of water rained down, covering all of them and the image became blurred. A tear had splashed on the picture he was holding. Joe sniffed and squinted his eyes tightly. Unfortunately he had returned to his attic, foot slightly throbbing from the splinter wound, and his throat hurting much worse. The lump begged to come out but a few hard swallows kept it at bay and only a few tears escaped.

Oh, what great times. Ah, time flies. God, I'd give anything to relive happier times again. Everything's changed so fast. Where did it all go?

Joe finished his pining for answers and laid the picture beside him on the pool table. *Keep this one out; put it somewhere... my desk, an end table, somewhere.* Then just as quickly as the beach scene had carried him away, he was ushered off again. Staring up at him from inside the makeshift treasure chest was the most beautiful smile he had ever seen. Her long hair was perfectly shaped and outlined her face, then came to rest on her chest; on the sweater he had given her for Christmas. It was their honeymoon. She had posed playfully on a balcony outside their room as he snapped the impromptu photo.

The lump returned and brought with it another round of memories. Again, he thought about happier times. He thought about their humble beginnings; about how dependant they were on each other. The memory caused him to consider the cliché that love outweighs all things.

We had nothing when we started out... not compared to now... and now we're caught up in striving to reach a more... comfortable rung of the ladder. Huh, if we knew then.... He tried to not let bad thoughts form. He shook his head a couple of times and tried to shut the door on it. Yet still, quick darts of bad memories rushed in as his mind shifted to some of their arguments over the years, and most recently, to the phone call from the day before.

She didn't mean it. We were both angry... my day was going terrible. Still, what she had said burned in his ears. Shaking his head again didn't stop her voice as it rang over and over in his thoughts. He grew angry, then calmed himself. *I know she didn't mean it. I said some mean words too.* Yet, the statement pressed on his emotions. He wasn't sure how to feel; both anger and heartache continued to surface. *I know we've both said it in anger before, out of frustration with each other, but...*

Then he discovered why her statement still pulled on his thoughts so much. *She said it so calmly.*

He replayed the argument as best he could remember, right up to the point where she calmed down and casually said, *'Joe, I think maybe we need to think about separating'.*

Perhaps the cool of the attic caused him to shutter or maybe it was the realization that as her calm statement replayed in his mind, he realized that he was still looking down at the photo. As he stared at her smile and innocent eyes, he couldn't help but wonder where she was.... *Where's she at now... and where is that determined, eager young man that snapped the picture? God, how we've changed.*

Time seemed to stand still as he reflected on the past two decades. Morose grew with each question that formed as contrasting images of then and now surfaced. Joy and sorrow fought viciously for Joe's emotions. Finally, the desire to return to the happiness that glowed from the photos won out. Like the final bell in a heavyweight boxing match, the sound of the front door slamming helped to end his emotional struggle. The next sound was of a car cranking.

She didn't bother to say good-bye.

Memory lane was now officially closed.

Thinking of the time, he snapped back to reality and turned to exit. Then the reason for his treasure hunt caught his eye. Shaking his head in astonishment, he thought, *that's why I came up here.*

Sitting on top of an old chest-of-drawers was a stack of books and on top of the stack was the study guide he had come for. It seemed as though it was beckoning for his attention as he was turning to exit.

How'd I miss that?

He shrugged his shoulders, then picked up the book, and the two memory-laden pictures, and headed out, closing the door behind him.

CHAPTER 7

FILTHY RAGS

"Sir.... Excuse me, sir", the man said.

The voice came from Joe's left, just outside his driver's side window. *Hurry* was the first thought he had. *Come on... go*, was the next. He was referring to the car in front of him waiting to pull out of the convenience store parking lot.

Don't look.... Look straight ahead. Joe was sure the voice was aimed at him as he waited his turn to exit. He sensed that someone was coming closer to his window so he gripped the steering wheel tight and reminded himself to not turn his head and acknowledge him.

Joe stopped here often to pick up a newspaper or grab a cup of coffee. Today he was just thinking about getting to work. He didn't have time to be nice to the homeless guy that sometimes held a sign at the exit of the store. He figured that was the source of his distraction. Joe's ride to work so far had been much like yesterday; excitement, bewilderment, and relief somehow all rolled together, and today, escalated emotions about his marriage. Naturally, the dreams perplexed his thoughts as well, but since leaving for work, he had begun swapping that mindset for the workday challenges that awaited him. He was sure another trying twelve hour day was ahead and he didn't want any distractions, like Godly dreams or his marriage, to get in the way of his focus on work.

I've got to get my thoughts and feelings geared up to tackle the challenges. I can't be dwelling on all this dream stuff. Joe thought how crazy it would sound to someone if he did end up telling his wife or anyone else. *Dream stuff? That's not really all of it…. The reading, the prayers*, he thought smiling. *I feel like I've talked to God the past few days.* Then he felt even odder as he wondered how that would sound to people.

Man, get a grip. This revelation stuff is great. Unbelievably great. But I have to focus on my job now.

If this guy doesn't go own…. Joe was starting to get angry at the wait and lifted his hand in preparation to lay down hard on the horn. As his hand started down, a startling sound got his attention. There was a peck on his driver side window and without thinking, Joe spun his head and saw him. The old homeless guy had tapped on the window and was leaned over with his face nearly touching it.

"Sir, your...", the homeless man started, but the jolt from being scared by the tap caused the rest of his statement to not register in Joe's ears, and he looked with puzzled amazement at the face in his window.

The man must have been just as puzzled as Joe, because they both froze for a few seconds without a sound and without moving. The car that had held up Joe's exit was now pulling across two lanes of oncoming traffic, across the paved section of median and left, just in front of heavy traffic. This section of highway was extremely busy, especially with the morning commuters.

The man's statement still didn't register with Joe and he thought it even odder that the stranger was calmly pointing upward with his index finger. The bony finger protruded through a torn end of an old, worn, brown knitted glove. He was still bent over with his weathered, whiskered face only inches from Joe's window.

What? What is he pointing at, bewildered Joe's mind as he snapped his head straight again and without any fore-thought, he pressed the accelerator hard, put both hands on the wheel and sped into the first two lanes of traffic. Fortunately, there was still an opening. Despite the rush of excitement and hurried exit, the thought, *filthy rags,* flashed in his mind as he started across the first two lanes, while still trying to orient his attention back on driving.

The homeless man was dressed in something that appeared to be more like layers of coats, or what used to be coats. His outer layer may had formerly been a trench coat, but now appeared more like strips of dirty cloth hanging from his shoulders. A mixture of colors, possibly from novice patch jobs, made it even harder to distinguish exactly what the old man was wearing.

Without looking down, Joe quickly reached for the console with his right hand to make sure his coffee cup was secure as he continued to turn sharply to his left and enter the flow of traffic, into the first lane, just on the other side of the median. The exclamation, *COFFEE CUP,* caused a sense of realization to punch Joe square in his stomach. The punch immediately induced nervousness. The next shocking realization trumped his first fear as sounds of screeching tires yelled to him from his right, reminding him that he had not checked traffic before speeding away from the would-be helpful stranger.

Without focusing on the screeching sound to his right, he quickly glanced and jerked the wheel violently to the left. As the screeching stopped, the sound of a car horn took the place of crunching metal and breaking glass that Joe expected to hear. Somehow there was not a collision. The driver of the screeching car yelled expletives at Joe as they swerved back into their lane and continued on. Joe's car came to rest in the grassy section of the median safely out of the way of traffic. His hands were glued to the steering wheel and his eyes shut tight. A few seconds seemed like hours as Joe tried to clear his head and calm down. He trembled in fear of what could have been, as the sounds of the crash he anticipated rang loudly in his mind. His hands went from the steering wheel to his forehead and then through his hair as he regained control of his racing breaths and waited for his heart rate to calm.

Traffic flow had returned to normal and his car shook with each passing vehicle just a few feet away. The sensation of someone staring at him caused him to look left, back toward the parking lot he had just exited. A quick re-trace of the past few seconds reminded Joe of the stranger, the unregistered statement, his pointing and finally, *my coffee cup.*

A relieving laugh jumped from Joe's chest and a big embarrassing smile crossed his face as he looked in the direction of the stranger. Then, the old man's statement registered in his thoughts loud and clear, only a minute or so too late. The stranger stood at the edge of the parking lot with an expressionless face, innocently extending a travel size stainless coffee cup in Joe's direction.

I left it in on the roof, Joe thought in regards to what the man had tried to tell him. *My coffee cup... he was pointing toward my cup on the roof.* Joe couldn't help but to laugh at himself again and shake his head. Then he motioned with his finger to tell the guy to wait a second, waited for an opening in the traffic, backed up, and pulled back into the parking lot.

"Thank you. Thank you so much", was the first thing Joe uttered to the stranger as he received his scratched coffee cup through the open window. "I must have set it on the roof as I opened the door", he continued, picking up the newspaper in the seat beside him, indicating that he had stopped by the store for a coffee and newspaper.

Without consideration, Joe invited him into his car. Degrading thoughts of his appearance; ragged clothes, old torn gloves, weathered face, and un-combed grey hair, were now replaced with compassionate questions and Joe wanted to help him. They drove a short distance and ordered breakfast at a McDonald's drive-thru and the new found friend graciously accepted the bag full of goodies that was handed to him.

There were many questions that burned in Joe's mind, like, *how did he get to this situation? Had he always been homeless? Does he have any family?* Out of consideration and respect, he chose not to ask but rather quizzed the old man as to what he could do to help him. As the new friend delighted himself in breakfast, Joe proceeded toward the inner city where he hoped to find a help center. As they drove, their conversation, interrupted only by large, anxious bites, provided Joe with avenues of discussion that he couldn't believe he was sharing.

Joe found himself answering more questions for his new confidant than vice-versa.

"So, these dreams, that you say you're having; you mean, they're like a movie of the Bible or something?"

The analysis amazed Joe. "Yeah, I guess so. You could say that they're a movie... except I'm in it and... real life is... somehow inter-twined."

As they criss-crossed the inner city, Joe found himself less eager to find the help center and yearning to share more of his experiences with him.

"Want me to hit another drive thru?" Joe asked, glancing at the empty bag in the guy's lap.

"No. No, thanks. Thank ya much though. That was good", he responded as he smiled toward Joe with biscuit crumbs clinging to his whiskers. "Just glad that car didn't take you out", he added, with a chuckle.

They shared a laugh as Joe admitted his mis-understanding about the coffee cup earlier, then sought to continue discussing his dreams and revelations. Joe was relieved to have a sounding board. He went on to confide that he was starting to find peace and answers through the Bible and prayer. In a contrasting manner, he began venting about his job and recounted the miserable workday from the day before prompting his new friend to say without hesitation, "then quit", causing Joe to look curiously at him.

"If you're so happy pursuing God and answers and finding your purpose, then just quit work. That's what I'd do."

Joe chuckled and rather than trying to explain that he has to provide an income, and the importance of having a job, he just nodded and agreed that maybe that would be the best thing to do. The simplistic answers and questions intrigued him to the point of losing track of time and direction. Finally, they reached their destination.

The old man thanked Joe again as they stood in the doorway of the shelter. Joe gave his new friend a piece of paper with his cell number and urged him to call as he made his way back to the parking lot. Just as Joe re-entered his car and prepared to insert the key, there was a sudden knock on the driver side window.

"HUH?" Joe gasped from startlement causing him to drop his keys. After the morning he had, Joe's nerves were on edge. The near-wreck, riding through town with a homeless stranger, and now a knock at the window as soon as he closed the door, caused a scare as if someone had thrust their fist through the window. Instead, he realized that it was only his homeless friend, leaning over, with his face only inches away.

How? How did he get back here so quick? He looked back toward the shelter door, some thirty feet away, then back to his friend. *Do they not watch these people closer? There's no way... did he follow me? He must've ran?*

His friend was holding something in his hand and gestured toward Joe to take it, nodding his head in Joe's direction. Without sparing time to fumble for the keys and roll down the window, Joe opened the door and the homeless guy reached around the glass and handed it to him.

A business card? Joe thought how odd it was as he peered down at the card he now held in front of him. He looked back toward his friend, still standing there smiling, and nodding reassuringly as if to say, 'go on, take it'.

With a blank expression, Joe closed the door once again, and reached down with his right hand to retrieve the keys. Still bewildered, he held the card in his left. As he inserted the key, he looked again at the card. It simply read, Angel Entertainment, Inc. with only a single name, Michael, in the lower left corner and the inscription, Hebrews 13:2, in the lower right. Joe shook his head in confusion as he cranked the car. As if looking for clues to make sense of it all, he flipped the card over and almost fainted.

Jesse!

On the back was handwritten the name Jesse and a phone number. Dazed and startled, Joe quickly looked up toward the entrance of the kitchen, then quickly to his left, then into the rear-view mirror, and then spun around to look out the back for himself. No one.

How did he go back in so quickly? Joe sat in a sea of perplexed thought. *Was this guy some sort of a sprinter back in his day or something?*

He couldn't have made it to the door that quick.

Again he spun his head around, looking out all sides of the car. To his left were two empty parking spaces and then the edge of the parking lot, entrapped by a chain-link fence. To his right was one empty parking space then a parked car, followed by a succession of ten or twelve parked cars, leading to a chain-link fence on the far side of the property. The entrance to the shelter was ahead and off to his right, centering the parking lot. A few worn picnic tables and benches were the only objects on the lawn area between the parking lot and the building. Behind him was the empty street. It was quite. As Joe gawked in all directions, he couldn't formulate an answer to his friend's disappearance. He tried to convince himself that he had made it back to the entrance before he looked up. Though the thought of something else occurring excited him. Quickly, he tried to remember if the guy had said anything strange or acted different; something that would signify what his mind had quickly formed.

An angel?

Possibly the week he had experienced thus far caused him to just accept the possibility. Or perhaps realizing how late he was for work caused him to shrug it off.

He had to have gone back in before I looked up. I didn't get the guys name, but it definitely wasn't the Jesse from the mall. Looked nothing like him. Wonder if this guy was Michael, Joe thought, in reference to the name on the front of the card.

With an amazed look on his face, Joe had no recourse but to exit the parking lot and head to work. It would not dawn on him until days later; after he began recounting his miraculous week, to look up the verse on the card. If he had done it sooner, then the latter, supernatural part of his week may have been more understandable. And possibly, not as terrifying when he would come face-to-face with a demon.

On the way back to finding the route that would lead him to work, Joe thought about how glad he was in helping the guy. Even if he felt obligated to, he still went through with it. He was happy in the good deed he had done. He also began thinking about the guy's simple answer, *'just quit'.*

Yeah, that would make life easier, he laughed, thinking about his debt, his wife, responsibilities, etc. Knowing that the suggested solution was not a viable answer to his work stress, he did ponder the old man's instruction's further and realized that work had been and could still be an interruption of his progress with God... to God.

The stress is for sure, he thought, in regards to the worst aspect of his job. He decided the simple instructions actually were his revelation for the day. *I have to quit letting work stress impede my real success.* The desire to read the Word returned to his heart as simple statements he had heard over the years in church suddenly made sense and echoed through his thoughts.

God is your provider.

Trust in the Lord with all thine heart and lean not unto your own understanding.

All things work together to the good of them that love the Lord....

On and on the revelations came. Like a kid given a surprise gift, Joe relished his thoughts. Suddenly, work challenges had a new perspective and Joe was glad.

My life is in God's hands; not my boss's, or the company's.... I'll continue to work hard but let the chips fall where they may. And with that revelation, Joe felt at ease and reached for the volume of his stereo. He wanted to add some *joyful Christian music* to his beaming happiness. Instead, what he got was yet another revelation.

"So DON'T you think for one second that man, in all his infinite wisdom, can do anything to affect his outcome", blasted from the speakers. The proclamation reminded Joe that he was normally at work by this time and evidentially preaching followed the morning serenade of contemporary music that he had heard the previous two mornings on the way to work. His curiosity perked and he listened intently.

"Isaiah 64:6 reminds us of this. But we are all as an unclean thing, and all our righteousnesses are as filthy rags; and we all do fade as a leaf...."

Filthy rags.... Joe recounted as the preacher continued, thinking of his reference to the homeless guys clothes.

"Yes, all the good deeds that you think you can do; in your whole entire life; if you worked day and night, tirelessly pursuing what you can do to help people; the community, elderly, homeless...."

Homeless, Joe thought.

"Would still not measure up. Your good deeds ARE as filthy rags when compared to the love of God's Gift; His Son; the One that provides eternal life. The love displayed in the brutal suffering, and death and resurrection of our savior IS the ultimate love story and NOTHING measures up to it!"

As the preacher paused to get his breath, Joe began thanking the Lord and uttering in amazement, "I get it... I can't believe it's never sank in... but I get it now. It's all about Jesus."

Then the preacher continued, "and the only thing you can do; what you should do, as a Christian, is fervently pursue God's will in your life. And the ONLY way to do that is to strive to live as Christ taught us."

Joe was stunned as he drove. His heart and mind absorbing the pastor's preaching.

The revelation continued, "Did Christ ever focus on Himself? Did Christ ever act in regards to His own well-being? Did He respond when He, Himself was mistreated or disrespected? Did He ever get angry?" The preacher paused and chuckled lightly. "Huh? You may have been answering 'no' and then stopped to think about that last question...." After another pause for the audience to reflect, it continued, "Of course He got angry.... In the temple. What made Him angry? What caused Him to respond? What was it that set Him off?"

The church people, the money. They were....

Before Joe could finish his thoughts, the speaker finished. "Jesus got angry at disrespect for His Father... our Father... our God... THE God. That's what set Him off; disrespect and dishonor for God. Think about it.... Even for Jesus, the Savior of the world, He had the same creed, the same motto that we are to have.... Not about me, but about Thee."

CHAPTER 8

ALL THINGS ARE POSSIBLE

Despite the long day at work, Joe decided to attend mid-week Bible study at his church. He had worked diligently to catch up after arriving late from his morning encounter and revelations. He worked right up to church-time and even later, as he tried to find a stopping point. Finally, he rushed toward the door. Earlier, his youngest daughter had phoned and informed him that she and her sister and mom would be stopping to eat on the way to church. Though it wasn't every week, his wife and kids usually attended mid-week service. The kids enjoyed youth group and their mother enjoyed the social circles that came with the typical ins-and-outs of planning activities. Regardless of why, the three attended more often than not. Joe had never found much interest in going, but tagged along if work allowed time or if there was enough energy left at the end of the day. This evening though, even with mental and physical fatigue, he desired to go.

On the way out of work, he grabbed a snack and soda from the canteen, to hold him over until he could eat supper. During the drive to church, while munching on peanut-butter crackers and wiping crumbs from his lap, he remembered what his daughter had told him.

Guess I'll pick up a drive-through burger on the way home.

For a second, the thought of rushed crackers, a fast-food supper, and fatigue, caused Joe to consider taking the turn that would lead him home.

Man, after the week I've had, I think I have the right to go home. Joe thought about Lazarus, about Jesse, about the boat. When the image of Denzel Washington flashed in his mind, he couldn't help but chuckle again and rationally think about his own sanity. He didn't really question his sanity but rather the whole aura of his dream encounters.

Should I talk to the pastor? Or someone at church? Has anyone else ever done this before? Wonder what they would think of me? Does God want me to do something or just keep going along for the ride?

Questions continued to surface as he drove, though he decided to go ahead and attend church.

Wonder if anyone would believe that the homeless man was an angel? Joe pondered his question. *Or could have been....*

Maybe I should just be quite about all this stuff for now, he decided.

He parked in the visitor parking space to save time walking to the door. After thinking one more time about how much of the night's service he had missed, he considered leaving.

I haven't been on Wednesday night in ages and now I show up when it's about over. Regardless of feeling dumb-founded, he shoved the car door shut behind him as he quickly headed toward the auditorium.

He crept in, trying to not disturb the quite setting, and set toward the back. The pastor's words seemed confusing as he tried to ascertain the origin of the study. He sat confused for a few minutes. The closest person was several pews away, so the thought of looking over someone's shoulder to determine the passage location was not a viable plan. A church Bible lay on the pew beside him, so he grabbed it up and waited for a hint of where to turn.

"You must understand that David had issues.... In today's society, he would have been considered really messed up", the pastor said.

Ah, David. Goliath story? Or King David, Joe wondered after hearing the pastor's words.

"Think about it.... Basically, forgotten by his father; 'go tend to the sheep'. The King ended up wanting him dead. He lusts after a married woman... has it arranged for her husband to be killed. On and on, we could talk about his characteristics. As my kids' might say, 'he was jacked up'."

The pastor waited for the audience to finish their chuckle, then continued. "But the one thing, that set David apart, was his desire... no, his passion, his burning essence inside him, was to love God.... Not just say that he loved God, but to really, earnestly, whole-heartedly, love and worship the Lord. As so many of the Psalms point out, just like Psalms 142; how he could have set down, while in the cave, and gave up, but instead, he penned such an amazing prayer...." The pastor paused.

"It's a perfect example. David poured out his heart to the Lord. He had trouble, seemingly on every hand. What do we tend to do? Most of us would have probably just complained.... That's why this study is so important; it's a living example of how we are to carry on. Don't quit talking with God when things get tough. Do as David did; pour out your heart to the Almighty loving Father.... He knows your heart and your thoughts anyway. Why not take time to talk with Him. That's what He wants you to do." Then he paused briefly before concluding.

"It worked for David. Maybe we should try it too."

Joe's wife found it odd that his car was at church and even odder that it was in the visitor's parking place. She and the kids had exited church before seeing Joe and were on the way home when he made it to his car. She called him as he was waiting in line at a drive through.

"What were you doing at church?" She asked.

Between trying to round up the correct change to pay the drive through attendant, pressing the phone between his ear and shoulder, and trying to answer their question regarding one or two packs of ketch-up, Joe responded in a frustrating, terse tone.

"I just went. Why?" He caught his tone as soon as the words came out, but it was too late. The only words that he had spoken to her all day came out all wrong and with the wrong attitude. He grabbed the bag of value-sized supper and pulled away from the window.

"I'm sorry, I....", he tried to add, but she interrupted.

"I'll see you at home.... I...."

He in turn interrupted as simultaneously they attempted to say, "I love you". Or at least that's what he thought she was going to say before he blurted it out. The phone went silent. He replayed the quick exchange again in his mind and considered calling her. He wasn't sure if she was going to say it, or if she did but his voice over-rode hers, or if she was trying to say something else. His appetite was gone and the nuggets were cold anyway. He felt around in the bag and realized that all the food was cold. *Just like my marriage*, he thought.

All three were readying themselves for bed when he came through the door. After a quick "love you" and "goodnight" to his daughters, he made his way down the hall to the bedroom. She was on the phone, so he just mouthed "hey" and offered a "goodnight", then motioned that he was heading back towards the den. She just nodded.

Despite feelings of remorse for the way he spoke to her, and disappointment with their relationship, he still had a desire to read. The pastor's lesson about David had pricked interests in Joe's heart to learn more. Though he had only heard a very small part of the lesson, his curiosity was guiding him down the hall, to the spare bedroom, and straight into more revelations.

After nestling into the chair in the corner, the first scripture he read was Psalms 142.

'I cried unto the Lord with my voice; with my voice unto the Lord did I make my supplication. I poured out my complaint before him....'

Complaint? We can complain?

'I showed before him my trouble. When my spirit was overwhelmed within me, then thou knewest my path. In the way wherein I walked have they privily laid a snare for me....'

Sounds a lot like work, Joe thought sarcastically, about many of the issue he faced on his job. Then he continued with verse five.

'I cried unto thee, O Lord: I said, thou art my refuge and my portion in the land of the living. Attend unto my cry; for I am brought very low: deliver me from my persecutors; for they are stronger than I. Bring my soul out of prison, that I may praise thy name: the righteous shall compass me about; for thou shalt deal bountifully with me.'

Wow... so he was in some sort of trouble, hiding in a cave, and this prayer brought him through.... Joe thought about some of the issues he, himself faced. He sat quietly, staring toward the wall but seeing nothing. The verses soothed him and he asked God to look upon himself the same way David had asked.

Then he decided to learn about David. He knew that if he got engrossed in a study that time could get away from him, but he chose to explore anyway. It was late and he had had a long day. With the help of his study guide, he turned to 1 Samuel 16 and began reading.

> 1 Now the Lord said to Samuel, "How long will you grieve over Saul, since I have rejected him from being king over Israel? Fill your horn with oil and go; I will send you to Jesse the Bethlehemite, for I have selected a king for Myself among his sons."

JESSE! What? Jesse? The name in verse one startled Joe. He read it again to be sure. He realized that if he knew the Bible better, then it wouldn't have been such a startling coincidence.

The same name as the guy in the mall....

Perhaps the name coincidence did it, or perhaps the heightened interests in learning did it, but instantly, revelations from the text leaped from the pages as Joe began reading.

At verse one, he questioned why God didn't just tell Jesse himself. *Why did he send Samuel to tell him that one of his sons would be king?* The thought that God's work is done through people came to mind. He's sure his pastor had said it before. Then, the thought that maybe God had been telling Jesse but he wouldn't listen came to thought. The quick revelations made Joe smile and he thanked God in his thoughts as he continued reading.

> 2 But Samuel said, "How can I go? When Saul hears of it, he will kill me." And the Lord said, "Take a heifer with you and say, 'I have come to sacrifice to the Lord.'
>
> 3 You shall invite Jesse to the sacrifice, and I will show you what you shall do; and you shall anoint for Me the one whom I designate to you."
>
> 4 So Samuel did what the Lord said, and came to Bethlehem. And the elders of the city came trembling to meet him and said, "Do you come in peace?"

At verse four; the mention of the elders trembling at Samuels arrival, Joe thought, *no need to worry when following God's command. He must have beamed with confidence as they trembled.* He read on.

> 5 He said, "In peace; I have come to sacrifice to the Lord. Consecrate yourselves and come with me to the sacrifice." He also consecrated Jesse and his sons and invited them to the sacrifice.
>
> 6 When they entered, he looked at Eliab and thought, "Surely the Lord's anointed is before Him."
>
> 7 But the Lord said to Samuel, "Do not look at his appearance or at the height of his stature, because I have rejected him; for God sees not as man sees, for man looks at the outward appearance, but the Lord looks at the heart."
>
> 8 Then Jesse called Abinadab and made him pass before Samuel. And he said, "The Lord has not chosen this one either."
>
> 9 Next Jesse made Shammah pass by. And he said, "The Lord has not chosen this one either."

10 Thus Jesse made seven of his sons pass before Samuel. But Samuel said to Jesse, "The Lord has not chosen these."

11 And Samuel said to Jesse, "Are these all the children?" And he said, "There remains yet the youngest, and behold, he is tending the sheep." Then Samuel said to Jesse, "Send and bring him; for we will not sit down until he comes here."

Man, his dad didn't even take him before Samuel. David must have had confidence issues right from the start, were the revelations that jumped at Joe as he read verses 11 and 12.

Suddenly, thoughts and revelations raced into his being so fast, that he struggled to grasp them all. He was comprehending the story so fully, that he felt like he actually knew David.

Did he whine and pout and stress over being left out. He was just left out there watching those sheep. Wonder if David lifted his own spirits by thinking about the story of Jacob? About Jacob going back to the rock at Bethel to renew his strength. Joe wasn't even sure how he remembered the story of Jacob.

When he read verse 13, about David's anointing, he thought how it may have been received; about how people may had doubted the choice.

'That can't be right. Surely God wouldn't pick that little one. That Samuel must be crazy.' Wonder how many church folk today would be the same way....

12 So he sent and brought him in. Now he was ruddy, with beautiful eyes and a handsome appearance. And the Lord said, "Arise, anoint him; for this is he."

13 Then Samuel took the horn of oil and anointed him in the midst of his brothers; and the Spirit of the Lord came mightily upon David from that day forward. And Samuel arose and went to Ramah.

Joe read the rest of chapter 16, and then read it again. The revelations and thought-provoking questions continued to come. Verse 20 caused him to say, "did Jesse finally get it now", regarding Saul's request for the Bethlemite's son that could play the harp.

He read verse 21. And David came to Saul, and stood before him: and he loved him greatly; and he became his armor-bearer.

Jesse finally sent David to the king. Is it possible that David was given the armor-bearing job so he could be around war and learn from it? And to be made tougher, mentally? All he had done was tend sheep. What did he know about war and being a leader?

That has to be why Saul was troubled and desired the soothing harp music; so David would have to be close to him at all times.... David was being prepared to be a warrior; a leader; a king, and at the time it would have looked like he was nothing more than a boy playing music and carrying armor.

WOW!, Jeremiah 29:11 fits David's life too!"

Joe sat back in his chair, completely blown away by the revelations. He read back over the verses again, trying to determine how the thoughts came to mind. Finally, he simply said in awe, *thank you Lord.*

In chapter 17, he read about Goliath, the Philistine and how the armies were squared off against one another. The mental image of verse 23 caused him to read it again.

> 23 And as he talked with them, behold, there
> came up the champion, the Philistine of
> Gath, Goliath by name, out of the armies
> of the Philistines, and spake according to
> the same words: and David heard them.

Wow. Did David get goose bumps as he saluted his brethren in verse 22, while hearing Goliath's challenge? Is it possible that right then and there, David had a twilight zone moment? Did he right then feel full affirmation that the time he had spent with Saul was not in vain? That the time since Samuel anointed him up until that very moment had been as God planned? I bet he felt an over-whelming sense of purpose and meaning.... But at the same time he had to feel a sense of fear.... I mean, the giant was undefeated; he was a killer, but yet at that very moment, God was telling David that his time had come.

Again, the scene played out vividly in Joe's mind. He could see this small shepherd boy, saluting his brothers and the rest of the army, and hearing the giant's challenge.

He had to have felt God's calling on his life as he internally answered the call.

The verse number, 23, caused Joe to think of the 23rd Psalm, so he turned to it and read.

David had to have been thinking about this very moment in time as he wrote this Psalm.... He had to!!!

1 The Lord is MY shepherd; I shall not want.

Joe pondered on how David compared his life with God to his job of caring for his father's sheep. He continued to read.

2 He makes me lie down in green pastures;
   He leads me beside quiet waters.
3 He restores my soul; He guides me in the
   paths of righteousness For His name's
   sake.
4 Even though I walk through the valley of
   the shadow of death, I fear no evil, for You

are with me; Your rod and Your staff, they
comfort me.

Joe's excitement jumped. *Yeah, I know he had to be thinking about facing the giant; about the decision to fight the giant. Man, this is awesome.... I can't believe I'm connecting these two parts of the Bible.*

> 5 You prepare a table before me in the presence of my enemies; You have anointed my head with oil; My cup overflows.
>
> 6 Surely goodness and lovingkindness will follow me all the days of my life, And I will dwell in the house of the Lord forever.

At verse 6, Joe realized that David must have still had fear about his task at hand, though he was brave enough to carry through with it. *David must have said 'win or lose, I'm your's Lord. Wow, how brave he was....*

Joe turned back to 1 Samuel, chapter 17 and continued reading.

> 26 And David spake to the men that stood by him, saying, What shall be done to the man that killeth this Phillistine, and taketh away the reproach from Israel? for who is this uncircumcised Philistine, that

he should defy the armies of the living
God.

WHAT? You got to be kidding me! David not only answered God's call, but is starting to sound confident. Joe bursts with enthusiasm.

He read the next verses quickly and excitedly, like he was approaching the end of a novel and anxiously wanted to know what happens.

> 27 The people answered him in accord with this word, saying, "Thus it will be done for the man who kills him."
>
> 28 Now Eliab his oldest brother heard when he spoke to the men; and Eliab's anger burned against David and he said, "Why have you come down? And with whom have you left those few sheep in the wilderness? I know your insolence and the wickedness of your heart; for you have come down in order to see the battle."
>
> 29 But David said, "What have I done now? Was it not just a question?"
>
> 30 Then he turned away from him to another and said the same thing; and the people answered the same thing as before.

31 When the words which David spoke were heard, they told them to Saul, and he sent for him.

32 David said to Saul, "Let no man's heart fail on account of him; your servant will go and fight with this Philistine."

At verse 32, he joyously concluded, *Oh, oh man, oh yeah, he's confident now. Yeah, he's almost sounding cocky; let me go get him. How brave.* The vivid images played out in Joe's mind like he was watching a movie.

33 Then Saul said to David, "You are not able to go against this Philistine to fight with him; for you are but a youth while he has been a warrior from his youth."

34 But David said to Saul, "Your servant was tending his father's sheep. When a lion or a bear came and took a lamb from the flock,

35 I went out after him and attacked him, and rescued it from his mouth; and when he rose up against me, I seized him by his beard and struck him and killed him.

36 Your servant has killed both the lion and the bear; and this uncircumcised Philistine will be like one of them, since

he has taunted the armies of the living
God."

37 And David said, "The Lord who delivered
me from the paw of the lion and from the
paw of the bear, He will deliver me from
the hand of this Philistine." And Saul said
to David, "Go, and may the Lord be with
you."

As Joe read verses 34 through 37, he started realizing more
about David's story; about how his time watching sheep,
while being ignored by his father, while his brothers fought in
the army, was still preparing him for his destiny. *God is... God*

38 Then Saul clothed David with his garments
and put a bronze helmet on his head, and
he clothed him with armor.

39 David girded his sword over his armor and
tried to walk, for he had not tested them.
So David said to Saul, "I cannot go with
these, for I have not tested them." And
David took them off.

40 He took his stick in his hand and chose
for himself five smooth stones from the
brook, and put them in the shepherd's bag
which he had, even in his pouch, and his

sling was in his hand; and he approached
the Philistine.

Joe didn't bother with the time. He was entranced in the story. He had known of David and Goliath since pre-school but never even dreamed that the story was so much more. Without pausing to reflect, he continued on his revelational journey. After reading verse 39 and 40, God poured out revelations to Joe.

David didn't try to fight man's way…. He trusted God. God will enable us and empower us to use what we have to do His work…. David's life experiences; his hobbies, his job, his desires, his passions, had led him to this very moment in time. He wasn't confused about what to do. He shed the conventional warfare; the armor, the sword, and trusted God to deliver him, with what he had to offer. Was David's earlier fear now replaced with peace and assurance?

Wonder if David felt like Paul did many years later; when Paul was dragged out of the city and left for dead. Did David and Paul both say internally, "well, whatever happens, I'm your's Lord…. All is well. Hey, what if Paul realized all of this about David's courage?

Joe continued to read. He understood the verses perfectly and the movie played in his mind. He was amazed.

Throughout the rest of the chapter, the revelations continued. David defeated the giant, just as the child-hood story told, but now, in his adult life, Joe discovered that there was much, much more meaning than just a youth that defeated an evil giant.

There were more revelations than Joe could remember but the over-whelming theme of them all, was that God provides all we need, when we need it, and if we trust Him completely, great things will happen... and great reward too. Verses 53 and 54 assured Joe of that!

Finally, the barrage of wonderful, awe-inspiring revelations came to an end for the night. Joe had to get some rest. He turned off the light and headed to bed. The week had been challenging, tiring, and inspiring. His mind jumped from one event to the next as he made the short walk down the hall, toward the bedroom.

Angels, dreams, preachers, homeless people, work problems, Denzel Washington... in a boat.... Joe laughed at the thought. *Jesse, Bible revelations....* Quickly the thoughts came to an end as he reached the bedroom and he became sad. He thought about the pictures from the attic as he momentarily stood in the doorway.

She must be sleeping on the couch again, he said to himself as he looked at the empty bed. Instead of climbing into bed, he knelt beside it and began to pray.

Even as he prayed, parallel thoughts of his week thus far still rang loudly. He prayed earnestly but still the amazing events of the week pierced his mind. It was Wednesday night. In some ways, Joe felt like the past 3 days had already lasted several weeks, yet in other ways, he wasn't sure if it had only been one long day; *one long puzzling, bewildering, inspiring day, or actually, one long… night.* Regardless, he was tired and needed rest:

The most fascinating parts of his journey still awaited him.

CHAPTER 9

REIGNING DOWN

"Ahh, man", Joe said in response to the statement coming from his cell phone. The workday had been just as brutal as the past two, except Joe weathered the stress with an assured sense that he was doing his best. Like yesterday, the day came without lunch. Instead of arguing or objecting, he desired to honor his boss's late morning request for an important document, resulting in him working straight through lunch, again. He realized that normally he would have felt annoyed at the last-second request, but somehow, today, he sensed that this approach was the way God would have him to respond. Joe worked feverishly to catch up and managed to have enough stamina to accept a friend's invitation for nine holes of golf after work. Though he seldom made time for golf, he didn't want to pass up on the opportunity today.

The person on the other end of the cell phone was a friend that Joe had not seen in a long time. Their families had spent a lot of time together over the years; cookouts, beach trips, and all the other things that similar families share. Their kids had played little league together up until his job took him to a nearby city about two hours away. They both were aware that two hours was not much distance, but with busy schedules, it might as well have been two days. Over the years, the contact had gradually become sparser and Joe couldn't remember the last time they had spoken until the call came in today. His friend was in town and wanted to spend a little time with his old buddy so they decided to golf when Joe finished his workday. With so many things on his mind, Joe had looked forward to the outing all afternoon as a chance to see his friend but also to relax a little. Joe was almost to the golf course when the cell call came that his friend would have to cancel their golf date.

"I'm sorry Joe, but I have to."

"No, no, that's no problem. Everything okay? You sound a little upset."

A brief pause caused Joe to look at his phone to be sure the call wasn't lost.

"Joe... the tests came back.... It may not be good."

"Oh, man, I'm sorry", was Joe's reaction but his mind raced to find the origin of the tests. *Did he tell me about any tests? I feel bad. I don't want to have to ask.*

"I told Kate I would hurry home."

"Yeah, I guess so. Exactly what I'd do." Joe hoped his voice didn't reflect his puzzlement as he spoke.

"I know I haven't talked to you in a while. I think the last time was a couple of weeks back when we first got the news that they may need to do a biopsy."

Suddenly Joe's heart sank. *Oh, gah, I forgot. How terrible and self-centered of me. I forgot all about it. Kate may have cancer.*

"Buddy, I'm so sorry."

"Yeah.. yeah, its... disturbing. But maybe it's not too bad. Kate sounded fine on the phone. She was very calm."

"Well, that's good."

"Yeah, we weren't expecting results till end of the week. They called her just now and said for us to come in in the morning."

"Well, what did they say on the phone?"

"Kate wasn't completely clear but she did say they assured her it would be okay...."

"Oh, thank God!"

"They did say we needed to go over the results. There will be some decisions to make."

"Well it doesn't sound too bad. Hopefully, it will be okay."

"Yeah, we're hoping and praying. When we know more, we'll call you."

They continued their conversation until Joe was parked at the golf course. He had continued to drive without thought and found himself parked at the course. After hanging up, he decided to go ahead and play. He felt compelled, even though it would be alone.

By the fourth tee, the clouds had quickly thickened up and a shower had rolled in. The cart had a roof and there was a thick grouping of large trees behind the tee box. After making an amateur weather prediction, Joe pulled under the tree limbs to wait out the quick passing shower. It only took a few more minutes for his eyelids to begin feeling heavy. The Pinnacle he was holding slowly slipped from his fingers and fell to the cart floor, then rolled off the side and onto the ground. Instead of the thudding sound awakening him, it catapulted him to another place entirely. A place that he would be glad he visited.

The rain is misting in under the roof of the cart, Joe thought. *The breeze must be causing the rain to lightly blow in on me.* Joe continued to think clearly while he slept. As if looking back toward the third hole green, Joe dreamt he heard crying.

What? Does someone need help? Sounds like a lady... or several people crying.... I don't remember seeing anyone playing behind me.... While still sleeping, he spun his head around looking for the source of the cries.

Where is it coming from?

In his sleep, he quickly surveyed his surroundings but saw no one. In reality, his head still dangled in front of his chest as he slouched in the cart seat asleep.

Then he heard another sound that puzzled him. It was coming from in front of him. He listened closer and heard it again. A mist of moisture sprayed his face again. He was intent on locating the origin of this sound and ignored the urge to wipe his face. He was sure the sound did come from in front but several feet above him. He sat motionless, listening. The padded cart continued to nestle him and he enjoyed his sleep, yet desired to pinpoint the source of the noise. The moisture lightly sprayed his face again and this time he brushed it off with his left hand several times to keep it from running into his eyes.

The deeper he fell asleep, the more he felt removed from the cart entirely. He thought about forcing himself to wake up and thought he had until the cries surfaced again.

Who is crying? As he strained to listen; to find the source of the despair, he realized there was multiple people in anguish. *Where are they?*

Then he heard the odd sound again. The one coming from directly in front and above. *It's so close, why can't I see it!*

He became frustrated. The sounds were so close but yet he saw nothing. Bewilderment joined frustration as he suddenly realized, *I want to wake up!* Before he could become more confused, another spray of moisture lightly covered his face. Instinctly, he reached up to brush it from his eyes, except this time he actually did physically move.

The cries got louder. The odd sound got louder. He was right in the midst of it. He demanded himself to wake up. His heart raced.

I've got to wake up!

Aggravation grew as he yearned to wake up. He wanted to see what was around him. The chorus of cries now enveloped him on all sides. He was in the middle of the crying multitude. The odd sound came again, followed by the mist on his face.

What is this? He said to himself regarding the mist.

Joe's confusion grew.

What is going on? He yelled to himself regarding the cries, and the sounds of agony.

Anxiety caused his heart to race faster. Nervousness caused him to perspire. Beads of sweat popped out on his forehead.

I've got to wake up! I've got to wake up now! Where am I? Joe yelled to himself to wake up.

The cries grew louder. The agonizing pleas continued.

Who? Who is hurting? Why are these people crying? Feelings of compassion set in.

After the odd sound and mist again, a sense of puzzlement and euphoria overcame him. He reached up to brush the moisture away. His left hand positioned over the left side of his face with his middle finger touching the inside corner of his left eye.

I feel odd... like when I dream about....

As his hand began to slide down his face, he finally, suddenly opened his eyes. Like a powerful beam of light, his eyes opened. He could see all around him. People surrounded him. The cries had faces. The sights caused him to jump in startling amazement. Quickly, he reached up with both hands to wipe his eyes again. Though perplexed and frightened, he wanted to see clearer. Hurriedly, his fingers brushed along his closed eyelids from the corner of his eye outward several times.

Perhaps it was the smell of it, or maybe the taste as it trickled into the corners of his mouth, or maybe it was both that caused him to begin to shake. Regardless of which sense triggered it first, Joe began to flush with emotions causing him to shake. Sensual, startling revelation of what the moisture might be caused him to pop his eyes open and slowly retract his trembling hands. Peripheral sights started registering and telling him where he might be. He knew for sure that he was definitely awake and more importantly that he wasn't at a golf course.

He managed to hold both hands about six inches in front of him. The sight coupled with the sounds around him caused him to gasp harshly. His mind told him what he saw but he wasn't sure to accept it. He wanted to, but he didn't know if he actually could.

Blood.

He struggled to get another breath as he quickly swiped his forehead with his right hand and returned it to its place beside his left hand, still only 6 inches from his face.

Blood!

Then the odd sound came again. Except this time it wasn't odd, or strange. The sound coming from in front, many feet above him was very clear now. He knew exactly what it was but still he wasn't sure if he was ready to accept it as reality. He continued to tremble. His heart pounded. His hands slowly, unconsciously lowered. His eyes widened and he felt entranced. He knew that euphoria must have been keeping him from passing out. Possibly, the dream trips he had encountered the past few days may have helped prepare him for the scene he was experiencing. The utmost sensations of love mixed with fear and amazement that enveloped him would have put a conscious Joe face first on the ground. As emotions buzzed through him like an electrical current, he realized that he wasn't standing, and he definitely wasn't sitting on a golf cart, but that he was already on his knees.

His eyes rapidly glanced to his left and right one time, and then focused squarely on the image he was gazing up at. The crying people were all around him and he was kneeling directly in the center of them, looking up in unison. Their sadness linked together. Joe's chest tightened like a stretched rubber band and his throat pained terribly. Tears gushed out as he cried out with them.

Oh dear Lord….

The sound again followed by the mist. Instead of reaching up to wipe at his face, his torrent sorrow caused him to double over in extreme anguish. Quickly, he righted himself. A mix of blood, sweat, and tears dotted his face and eyes causing him to squint hard. He didn't want to miss anything and it was starting to get darker.

Oh my God! He's struggling to breathe.

The sound came again and it was all clear to Joe now. A struggling, suffocating sound is what he had been hearing. The noise that sounded odd before was no longer misunderstood. It was a gasping, quivering sound.

Then came the mist raining down on the crying crowd. A mist of blood and sweat showered them.

Entranced in utter amazement, Joe's senses told him again that he was really there. *I'm at the foot of His cross….*

Joe desired to get to his feet but knew he probably couldn't. He trembled. His agonizing heartbreak was fueled with extreme guilt. Pity and compassion aided in his unattainable desire to help Him. Though he knew how the scene would end; how this was God's great and merciful plan and that despite the pain and agony, it was Jesus' passion, Joe still yearned to do something.

In sorrowful, sobbing, broken thoughts, interrupted by his own gasps for air in between cries, Joe sought for help. *If I can get to his legs.... If I can grab them.... If I can push him up.... I can help him breathe....*

As Joe struggled to formulate his plan, it happened again.

Jesus strained to pull Himself up. He writhed in pain as He managed to lift His sagging body up for another breath of air.

Dear God, this is horrible.... He's suffocating.

Then finally, the awful, gasping, quivering intake of oxygen. Jesus had pulled himself up and got one more breath. Then just as unmercifully, His legs gave way and he fell back down causing a violent exhale. The cross shook and wobbled as His body dropped downward, his arms stretching terribly. Blood was streaming down his face. What was left of his beard was saturated with it. The force of Him dropping back down caused a violent exhale that showered Joe again with a mist of blood.

Joe cried uncontrollably. He cried so hard that he hurt. His arms crossed his torso and pressed against his abdomen as if in extreme pain. The anguish of seeing it all was more than he could bare. Being literally showered with His blood paralyzed his thoughts. He couldn't believe it. He was awestruck and unable to process any mind activity for a few seconds. His head hung. Then overwhelming shame and guilt made him momentarily desire to be carried away; for it to all be over, though he knew he should look. Somehow he managed to look up again.

The crown, the blood... He's covered in blood.... It's horrible.... God, they beat him.... So badly....

It became darker and it was harder for Joe to see more details. Suddenly, all sound vanished and the air was completely silent. It seemed like the entire crowd around Joe was gone. There was not a sound. No one was at the cross but him. Joe sensed that his experience was about to end; that he had only seconds left to witness the ultimate sacrifice. Then Jesus lifted His head just enough to look directly at Joe.

"I did this for you, Joe", the Savior said. "So you can know the Father's love as I do. I am your friend, your confidant. Believe in me and know that I want to shower you with love and happiness. Draw closer to me and I will draw closer to you. Share me with the world; your world; the ones in your life. Brag on me and show others what I am for you and I will lift you up and bless you with a life more abundant. As I said before, you will do greater works than me.... Draw close to me, Joe. Make living with me your focus, the pinnacle of your desires and I will pour out my blessings upon you."

Perhaps it was the desire to cry out louder or perhaps the crack of thunder that brought Joe back to the golf course. Regardless, he was back. Though the weather was now a strong storm, and he needed to seek better shelter, Joe couldn't move. He sat motionless, and cried. He didn't care about the weather or anything else. He just wanted to keep absorbing the words that Christ had told him. They chimed through his thoughts over and over. He buried his face in his hands and cried. It may have been as much as an hour before he tried to move from his slumped position on the cart. Like a photographer analyzing pictures, he burned images into his mind, wincing and shaking his head in astonishment at the pain He endured, as each mental snapshot surfaced. Finally, he retreated back to his car; somber, amazed, astonished, and yet completely engulfed in a sense of love and peace and contentment like he had never felt.

It was well after supper time when he arrived home. He ate only a few bites of left overs, told his family goodnight and went to bed. He didn't pray but instead thanked the Lord over and over as he quickly fell asleep. Perhaps it was due to the intense level of his most recent experience or possibly he was just simply that tired, but the night's sleep was sound and un-interrupted.

CHAPTER 10

THE FINAL CHAPTER

"Jesse! I have to see you.... I'm sorry, I've got to talk to you. I mean... I need to talk to someone... and I would rather talk to you than anyone." Joe yelled frantically in his cell phone, his hand trembling and beads of sweat popping out on his forehead.

"Joe... that you?"

"Yeah, I just... you want believe what's happening...."

The reality of actually speaking with Jesse startled Joe but he was thankful it was really him. Realizing Jesse wasn't a dream provided a small amount of relief from the nightmare he was experiencing. Calling the number on the business card and hoping it was his mall friend was desperate, but Joe needed help. The potential for making an embarrassing mistake didn't alter his opening panic-stricken requests. Things had suddenly escalated to an unbelievable new level. The dreams, the revelations, the inter-twining of reality and dreams had all been an amazing ride, but now, today, was something totally different. It was horrifying.

The day had started normal enough. Today was Friday and despite the life-altering week, Joe was looking forward to a restful, yet eventful weekend. Just an hour or so before, Joe had had difficulty praying. He could not believe the fortune that had befallen him. It was all he could think about. He tried to concentrate on the topics he needed to cover in his prayer but instead of progressing from thanking the Lord first, and then into his needs, he hung up on thanking Him. Every time he started into his prayer list, he sensed that his Father already knew the list of needs, and all he could muster in verbal thoughts was, "thy will be done". Over and over, he said it and found himself repeating it in different ways. He prayed God's will in all areas of his life and delighted in the simplicity of the talk with his Father.

Joe cried joyful tears as he sensed that God was comforting him and saying, "just sit in my presence this morning and rest while we talk". The solitude soothed Joe in every way possible, as he wondered if God was kind of telling him that it had been a long week and was pleased with the steps he had made on his journey. *What an amazing week* rang loudly in his mind.

As continuing his morning prep for work, he thought back to a week earlier and the memory of his mental and psychological state seemed like a lifetime ago versus the spiritual euphoria he bathed in this morning.

Not only was the end of the workweek gratifying but Joe had other reasons he was glad Friday had arrived. His wife was going to be surprised with flowers at work and a card reminding her of their dinner plans at her favorite restaurant. Joe had planned it the day before. They needed some time alone to talk and start recovering their relationship. He wasn't sure how he would introduce her to his amazing week but he yearned to tell her and knew that his personal recovery would aid in their marriage recovery.

Suddenly, his thoughts and plans had taken a back seat to his present experience. On the way to work, he thought he had seen something strange and now he was sure he had. A young boy about seven or eight had escaped death or serious injury when he lost control of his bike and stumbled from the sidewalk in front of the car ahead of Joe. Joe had gasped loudly in fear when he was sure the boy would be run over. Except, at the last minute, someone had reached from the sidewalk and pulled the boy back upright and out of the path of the car. The man with the saving hand seemed to come from nowhere and disappeared just as quickly. Joe saw the man seemingly vanish as he watched in his rear view mirror while pulling around the stopping car in front of him.

The scene was so amazing that Joe had no course of thought except to admit that it may have been an angel that saved the young boy. As unbelievable as it sounded, Joe just couldn't come up with another answer.

The perplexing thoughts from witnessing an apparent angel appearance had been replaced by emotions from an equally amazing event, except it induced fear; strong, gripping fear. Joe was now in his car at a fast-food restaurant, trying to back out of a parking place while urgently calling Jesse.

A minute before, he was standing in line, patiently waiting his turn to order, when the day turned horribly dark.

"Ma'am, I'm sorry but the coupon has expired", the lady behind the register said. Joe was second in line and due to the escalating confrontation that had been brewing ahead of him, he had taken a few steps back.

"You GET your manager... NOW, you stupid...."

Thankfully, Joe thought, the customer stopped short of continuing the degrading statement, hopefully indicating that she would calm down.

"Ma'am, I can....", the employee started, only to be rudely interrupted.

"I TOLD you to get your manager. That's all you need to do, you..."

This time the irate customer continued with a derogatory, insulting name and Joe desired to intervene. Without hesitation, Joe spoke up. "If you would quit urging her on...."

Before he could finish, he realized something was different; horribly different. Trembling fear overtook Joe. An awful despair enveloped him. A fright a thousand times worse than he had ever experienced smacked him in the face and quickly suffocated him with a presence of evil. The man he spoke to was whispering bad thoughts and words into the lady's ear right in front of him. The instigator was only an inch or two from her, except it wasn't a man. It wasn't even human. Joe was terrified.

"GET OUT!" Graveled from its voice as it reacted to Joe and spun in his direction. Joe immediately started falling backward as it lunged at him. Its mouth was open wide. A tangible, visual presence of evil was attacking Joe. Its mouth was opened wider than a human could open and the teeth were jagged, pointed fangs. A creature straight out of hell was attacking Joe. The eyes were blood red and pierced him with evil and Joe felt it. The skin was gray and resembled wrinkled paper. Sores like boils covered its face and hairless head. Its presence towered over Joe as he fell back to the floor. A demon was attacking Joe.

"GET OUT!" Screeched from it again as it bent over the top of him as he fell backwards. Joe was frozen in fear.

Later in retelling the account, he wasn't sure how he had escaped. The only thing he could surmise was that despite the paralyzing fear, he managed to catch his fall with his hands thrust behind him. Then spun to his side without thought and bolted toward the door.

"I can't believe it! YOU GOT TO HELP ME!" Joe shouted in his cell phone. He had made it to his car parked in front of the door. The ominous business card was in the console. Joe had dialed the number written on the back of it while frantically cranking the car.

Back inside the restaurant, everyone gazed in shock at the crazy man that ran to his car for no apparent reason. They remarked that he must have slipped and fell and ran from embarrassment.

"I've been waiting on you to call", came from the phone.

"So you ARE... this is... the Jesse... the one I met....", Joe stammered from fear and rush of adrenaline and nervousness. His quest for breath interrupting his statements. He threw the car in reverse and quickly turned his head to look over his right shoulder.

"I NEED... your... help!!!!" Instead of speeding backwards, he instantly slammed the brakes, halting his retreat from the parking space. The instinct that someone was watching beckoned at him. His thoughts raced. He knew not to look. He knew he had to speed away from his deathly encounter, but he couldn't resist. Decisions rushed through his mind in a split-second. Conscious desire was to run but the subconscious called for his attention.

LOOK!

He spun around to his left and saw it again. Less than an inch away, on the other side of his driver side door, it was hunched over snarling at him. It had followed him. He was face-to-face with the demonic presence again. Its lifeless breath wetting the window as its fangs dripped some sort of slimy saliva.

HURRY! GO, was the only thought as Joe threw his right arm toward the backseat and spun his head away from the monster to look out the rear window.

"NOOOO!" Joe shouted. A car had stopped behind him, temporarily blocking him in. He spun back around shouting.

"NOOOO!" His pleas for help were coming without thought. His mind formed hundreds of images and conclusions in hyper speed. *Back up anyway, jump out of the car, get someone's attention, yell for someone, shove the door open, a gun, I wish I had a gun, how can this be real....*

What happened next convinced Joe that he was going to die.

All his thoughts and pleas and desires to escape ceased instantly. He spun back around, grabbed the bottom of the steering wheel with both hands, slammed his eyes shut and waited, like the prey of a firing squad. His only plight was, *I WANT TO LIVE!!!!*

The car started rocking side to side violently. The demon shook it with furry. Awful, terrible sounds came from it. The driver side tires left the pavement, then thudded back down. Over and over again. Joe held tight to the steering wheel in hopes of not being tossed back and forth in the front seat. It was trying to turn over his car.

"GODDDD! HELP ME! JESUS, PLEASE!

Immediately the car set squarely on the ground before Joe finished shouting his pleas for help.

"Oh God, God, what...." Joe opened his eyes, breathing frantically, and then slowly released his death clutch of the steering wheel. Instant memory of his hesitation just a few seconds earlier bulged in his emotions. He spun around desperately searching all sides of the car for the being. His breathing continued to race, his eyes wide, and hands trembling. "What is going on? What is happening? Why...." He asked in many variations as he tried to gain his composure. The car had moved from behind him and Joe slammed the gas to back up.

Then he heard, "Joe, Joe, talk to me. Joe."

Looking down to his lap, he suddenly remembered, *JESSE!!!!.* With a relieving exhale of panic-stricken breath, he picked up the phone that had fallen to the seat between his legs during the attack.

"Joe!" Jesse said again as Joe put the phone to his ear and held it in place with his right shoulder. His left hand steered the car and the right one slammed the shifter into drive as he made his aim for the exit.

Grabbing the phone again with his right hand, he yelled, "JESSE... I got to talk to you. SOMEBODY. Anybody. Just help me, please.... You seem like who I need", his breathing still frantic, "I mean, I guess, will you, can you...."

Jesse interrupted, "JOE. Joe, I'm here. Are you okay?"

Joe looked around his car, then in the mirrors.

"Yeah... uh, yeah, I think. I guess... I don't know. Maybe. I can't believe this."

"I'm here for you. It's okay. Just calm down", Jesse said in a peaceful, reassuring voice.

"Can you meet me...."

"Just go home and we'll talk there", Jesse interrupted. Then the phone went silent. Joe held the phone in front of him and looked at the display, then threw it in the seat beside him and raced home.

Arriving home, he threw the car in park and rushed through the front door and quickly turned the corner of the hall. He ran almost without thought, as if he had never been in his house before. He caught himself stopping at his bedroom entrance as if he thought Jesse was there. With a quick spin, he ran back down the hall, past the other bedrooms, slid to a stop on the area rug, then it him.

MAN! What am I doing?

OHHH, man, how stupid. He doesn't know where I live, he yelled to himself turning around to run back to his car to retrieve his cell phone. He jerked open the front door, threw it aside and ran through the opening and into the outstretched arms that greeted him.

"JOE! JOE! STOP!"

He struggled to stop his momentum and collect himself without knocking them both to the porch floor. The object in front of him was big and weighty enough to withstand his charge. Immediately, he knew who it was before his thoughts could fully put the revelation together.

Sweat glistened his forehead and his face was blood red as he began to focus on the sight in front of him. Despite the startling surprise, Joe welcomed the stranger's support.

"It's okay. Just try to calm down.... Come on.... Gonna be okay".

Joe and Jesse stood face to face, only an arm-length apart. Bewilderment and relief flashed in Joe's eyes as Jesse lavished him with assuredness while supporting him with arms extended and hands resting on his shoulders. Joe heard his consoling tone and realized that soothing dialogue was being offered but the loving, comforting expression offered by the mall stranger was sinking in a lot more than the words. They stood face-to-face without moving, except for Joe's chest pounding as he tried to catch his breath.

"Let's get in here and get ya a drink of water", Jesse said, motioning for them to re-enter the house. But Joe still stood motionless as he continued absorbing the appearance and stature of his mall friend; the grandpa-esque stranger that offered wisdom just a few nights before. Anxious questions leaped to his thoughts with every pounding pulse of his racing heartbeat. He quickly put aside the escalating desires for answers as he yearned to remember details of the mall stranger that he unsuspectingly chatted with earlier in the week; the stranger that was now a welcomed embrace on his front porch.

Amongst the chorus of questions and thoughts fueled by adrenaline coursing through him, and despite the euphoria-like confusion that was now overtaking him, Joe realized something else was happening. The wisdom-filled stranger that offered the verse from Jeremiah was now, several days later, offering the only sense of normalcy that he had experienced all morning long. And the normalcy was being conveyed with a simple, loving, reassuring smile. While calmness continued to set in, Joe began accepting that this grandpa person was real; that their conversation in the mall had been real; that this morning was real, and that he really was seeing Jesse again. Despite numerous questions and confusion, Joe knew instantly, without any further thought, to put all of it aside and forego desire for immediate answers and just follow the instructions Jesse offered. That conclusion offered the most solitude but still he realized it was odd to ignore the quest for logical answers, especially given what he had experienced thus far today, but he found peace in yielding to Jesse's suggestion. His breath began coming back to him and he turned to go back inside the house. As he obediently began to turn, there was still one question he couldn't put aside. Perhaps it was what he saw in his driveway that almost caused him to spin back toward Jesse and demand answers. Or more appropriately, maybe it was what he didn't see that tempted his anxiety to build again.

Only my car.... How did he get here?

Jesse motioned them to the kitchen table, continuing to console him with an all-knowing, all-caring peaceful demeanor that only a grandpa-figure like Jesse could display. His calmness invoked peace in Joe as he seated him at the table before stepping into the kitchen. He hummed quietly while non-chalantly opening and then closing cabinets. He progressed from the far left side of the kitchen where the cabinets start, then past the stove and continuing again, cautiously peeking inside each one, then closing it. Joe watched patiently before realizing he must have been searching for drinking glasses.

"I'm alright Mr. Jesse. That's okay. I'm gonna be okay. I'm beginning to feel a lot better now." Even as he finished his words, the mystery of the demon returned to his thoughts. The image caused him to quickly shake his head as if trying to jolt some sense back into himself.

A demon?

I'm not okay. I don't know who Jesse is... or how he got here.... *Or....*

Realizing there were so many questions, he decided just to sit patiently and wait on Jesse. He sensed it was the right thing for him to do. Simultaneously, he realized it seemed like the only thing he could do as well.

"Here ya go", Jesse said as he sat a glass of water on the table in front of Joe. Then he pulled a chair up close, just to Joe's left, within arm's reach. As he sat down, he continued to exuberate peacefulness. His expression assured Joe that he was protected and in good company, despite the questions he had. After taking several deep swallows of water, Joe lowered the glass and sighed in relief. Jesse sat patiently, still smiling, like a care-free grandpa sitting on a park bench enjoying a warm sunny day. After a few seconds, Joe sensed he was waiting on him to start talking. Scenes from the attack flashed in his mind, as if he was watching a replay of himself being assaulted by the demon and frantically calling for Jesse on his cell phone. He took a deep breath and started to talk.

"I never thought I would ever see what I did while ago", Joe said while sitting the glass down on the table, then dejectedly leaning back in his chair and lowering his head. "It was horrible."

"There's really no other way to put it...." Joe said, looking back up at Jesse to get his reaction.

Then he continued slowly. "It was... a demon", then he hesitated.... "No doubt...." Shaking his head in disbelief, he pressed on, "I was attacked by a demon...." Then as if doubting what he knew was fact, he added, "Uh, a... demonic presence... or something. I don't know", he said shaking his head as he leaned forward and looked down.

Still Jesse sat with the same expression and demeanor. Like he may have already heard the story before. Joe looked at him puzzlingly, then continued.

"Well, first of all, the day started out odd to begin with. I can't believe I'm actually saying it but... well... I know what I saw, and if this sounds too weird...."

"No, go on." Jesse said, biting his bottom lip tenderly, and widening his eyes. Joe thought it was as if Jesse already knew the story.

"This kid... was on a bike, and I know the only way he was not killed was because an angel reached out and saved him.

I know that's what happened. He was on the sidewalk, lost his balance, and fell.... Right in front of a car and this, this, person, suddenly reached out from the sidewalk and pulled him back upright." Joe paused and glanced up at Jesse again, then around the room, not stopping to focus on anything, but blindly searching for the next sentence.

"Joe." Jesse said reaching out and placing a hand on his shoulder. Then pausing to gather his full attention.

"Don't you think you saw something that happens everyday.... Everywhere.... The fact is, spiritual warfare happens all the time. You think it's possible that somehow you were allowed to see it? Visually." Then he raised his brow in an all-knowing gesture, like he did in the mall and answered his own question convincingly, "I think so".

Then Joe continued recounting his morning as Jesse patiently listened, offering reassurances along the way. When Joe reached the part that he shouted for God's help and the attack ceased, Jesse spoke up again.

"The Book says that evil has to flea if confronted by the name of Jesus Christ".

Joe looked up quickly from his blank stare toward the floor. "Yeah, that is what happened", Joe replied. *That has to be what happened.* "But... why...", stuttered Joe, "did this happen to me?" Then he peered toward Jesse, yearning for answers.

"Heee", Jesse chuckled, "you've been on one amazing journey haven't you."

"Yea.... Definitely! I have". Then Joe paused to think, *what does he know?* "And this morning I was sure that I had come a long way." As he finished speaking, he had already formed the thought, *how much did I tell him at the mall?*

"And it sounds like you have", interrupted Jesse. Joe's thoughts about what his mall friend knew about him momentarily overrode the conversation and Joe gazed curiously past Jesse causing Jesse to say again, "I'd say you have experienced a lot recently; your revelations, your dreams..."

"You see, it's just that, well, I... I'm just not sure where I'm at.... That verse you gave me.... It's like it goes along with these dreams, and... revelations...", Joe cautiously searched for the right words to say, "that I keep having. And not just dreams, like at night, but while I'm reading the Bible too. It's like it's all so... real now. I read the Bible and it's like images come to me without even thinking it.... Like I'm seeing it all come to life."

"You see, Mr. Jesse", continued Joe, "I've been searching for purpose... in life. I don't mean to sound ungrateful... I am thankful for my family and the responsibility of caring for my family, but... I've... I've just been... miserable. The past couple of years, or longer.... I don't know, maybe less, I've not really been able to say when, but I guess it's just been building up. I have been so low... so unfulfilled... so down... so depressed...

like there's really no meaning for my life. At least nothing of importance, anyway. I used to have hobbies... and I've always been a simple-to-please type person.... I used to enjoy simple things... like just relaxing on the porch with a cup of coffee.... But now, well at least up until this past week, I have been constantly unhappy.... And it doesn't pass. I mean I try not to... mope around, but I'm just so... so, empty, I guess. I never feel happy." Joe paused and looked down, then, took a deep breath while looking up again. After a long exhale, he continued, "and I don't think I'm off base in saying that I just don't believe that... that... is how life is supposed to be; just empty and trivial. Does that make any sense?"

Jesse smiled bigger and just slowly nodded his head in assurance.

Joe reached for the glass of water again. As he took a drink, he realized how quite and solitude the house sounded. The time was approaching mid-morning and everyone was at school or work, except for him. *I'm sitting at my table pouring out my troubles to someone I don't know.* As odd as it sounded, Joe felt assured that he was in good company and continued his story.

"You hear so many stories about rich people; athletes, movie stars, business people, on and on... that realize that money and material things don't satisfy them.... They become blasen. Or stories about people that did great achievements... like the superbowl winning quarterback from several years back that later admitted to having a feeling of 'is this it?, is this supposed to be so great?' while he was still on the field, you know? Or like the astronaut that walked on the moon; you hear that he was depressed because he thought he could never accomplish such great goals again."

After pausing to catch his breath, Joe continued. "I mean, it's not like I have a prominent role in society like the people I mention but I can relate to them... at least from the standpoint of being unfulfilled. It had got to the point that I felt so, so... empty, that I had no emotions left in me. Things that used to satisfy me, no longer did...."

"Go on." Jesse smiled bigger again.

"At least until this past week...." Joe stared out the window, then back at Jesse. "I've been having dreams and revelations from the Bible. Things I've never experienced. And the more I dig into the Bible, the more of a sense of... of, like, relief, and joy, and... hope". Joe paused and let the words soak in a minute. *Hope. Yeah, that feels good to say again.*

"It's been so great, but... also this week... I've experienced bad stuff too. Bad news... and challenges and disappointment at work. Issues with my marriage too. Stuff that seems like it's actually a little worse than before. Before, I was kind of just trudging through life; down and out and miserable, but at least not being confronted with harder challenges and heartaches.... I just don't understand."

Then Jesse finally spoke up.

"Have you ever wondered if maybe we're not supposed to understand everything?"

Joe leaned back in his seat ready to take mental notes of grandpa's teaching. Then Jesse said it again to add emphasis.

"Have you ever wondered if maybe we're not supposed to understand everything?"

"Have you ever thought that if we ever 'figure out' God, then maybe He wouldn't be God? It's like then we would be equals?" Jesse chuckled at himself and continued.

"The Bible says 'a lamp unto my feet'. Think about that a second.... It means, that we are to trust God. That He is our way, our truth, and our life. All we are required to do is trust that he will give us our next step.... He lights the next step, not the path... not the whole... journey... just the next step.... That's all; trust Him to show you the next step and most of all, trust and believe, without wavering, that he knows all the steps... for your whole life. If you'll just let him be your God. Regardless of what you are experiencing or going through... that's just it... if you put all your trust in God, you will 'go through'.... He will NEVER leave you, nor forsake you.... Never. Even when you feel like He may have... never, Joe, never, does He leave you. You can't comprehend what God has for you and why you face the things you do.... Next step, that's all you have to do.... Keep taking that next step."

Silence filled the room for hours. No one moved. At least that is how Joe felt. His mind tried to move him from focusing on the topic; on the very essence of understanding what he needed to know in order to be.... He wasn't sure how to finish his thought. *Be... happy?* The simple word paled miserably in describing his soul's core desire. Joe knew that he was experiencing more. Much more than a lesson in happiness. *Contentment?* He thought, then paused and stared aimlessly. Again, his mind tried to interrupt his plight for description. *The kids? Dear? Is she okay? What time is it? Work! I have to go.... NO!* His super-ego slammed the door on further rambling thoughts. *The rest of your life is hanging in the balance.* The thought seemed too dramatic... even for this morning. *No, it's not too dramatic*, he argued to himself. Jesse seemed to no longer be in front of him. Joe's eyes circled and darted. His breathing intensified again. His inner argument was taxing. He was not being a good host. Jesse sat patiently without a word; without movement. Joe wanted to bring himself back to reality. Or wherever he was at the moment. Finally he gave up. He gave up on searching for the word, or explanation for what he was experiencing. Like forgoing resistance to a desire, like giving in and having desert, or splurging for the larger purchase, the bigger tv or the fancier car, Joe finally snapped back to.... Wherever he was. The remainder of his life hung in the balance.

Joe caught himself leaning up on the edge of his chair like a child listening to a captivating children's story. He desired to hear more; to understand more.

"So you desire fulfillment... and happiness... and purpose in life?"

Joe nodded.

"Ultimate fulfilling of purpose and an aura of fulfillment comes through sincere personal growing to God."

Jesse paused for Joe to reflect on the statement. At first, the sentence seemed cliché, but as Joe said it again to himself, *ultimate fulfilling of purpose and an aura of fulfillment comes through sincere personal growing to God,* he realized that it was exactly what he had experienced the past few days. Jesse saw the revelation in Joe's expression and continued.

"Whosoever believes in Him...", then Jesse seemed to catch himself and add, "do you believe?" His eyes seemed larger than his smile as he peered into Joe's stare. Joe was fully entranced into Jesse's question.

Joe nodded, prompting Jesse to request, "then say it; 'I believe'".

Obediently Joe replied, "I believe". His eyes grew wider and his heart raced.

Like an elementary school teacher gently nudging a timid student in the right direction, Jesse asked, "you believe what?"

Joe knew the answer but struggled to put the response together. "I believe... Him. In Him." His eyes squinted, he bit his bottom lip, letting it slowly slip from between his teeth. The eyelock with Jesse broke. His mind wandered for a second and he blankly stared, then continued with more assurance as he resumed eyelock with his teacher, "I believe in Him, the Christ".

Jesse added, "Christ, God in man-form. You believe?"

Joe answered, "I believe!"

Immediately, somewhat demandingly, Jesse responded, "then believe His Book!"

Jesse froze, without blinking. He let his command penetrate Joe's being. Silence. He waited a few more seconds before continuing.

"BELIEVE", Jesse's voice raised as he started. "Belieeeeve", he repeated, stretching the word, "that you have a better life, a rewarding life, a fulfilling life, a joyful life, a hopeful life, an abundant life. Believe! That it's there for you.... If you will take it!"

Sounding like a courtroom lawyer's counter argument, Jesse jumped on top of his previous statment. His voice raised yet again, "WHY NOT? Why not believe? Why not believe HIS Book?" The eyelock continued and without hesitation, Jesse drove home his argument. "WHY believe anything at all if not going to believe it all?"

As if holding a book, Jesse held his hand open in front of Joe and poked his palm with his index finger. "He said, right here, in His Book" then repeated it, "right HERE, in HIS Book, he says it, 'a more abundant life'. Do you believe it Joe? Grab hold and believe it; accept it." Jesse added again, "Believe!".

"I do. I believe", Joe answered emphatically, nodding his head in agreement.

"His Book says, 'for with the heart a person believes, resulting in righteousness, and with the mouth he confesses, resulting in salvation', and it also says, 'whoever believes in Him will NOT be dissapointed'. Ha, that's pretty good ain't it Joe? You feel dissapointed Joe?" Jesse smiled and leaned back in admiration of the scripture.

Joe smiled and shook his head. His eyes seemed a bit softer now; less intense than before. He felt relieved.

"Joe, can you say that now? Can you say with your mouth, as the Book states, that Jesus is the Son of God? And that God raised Him from the dead?"

"Yes, yes! I do. I say it. I can say it. I believe it." Joe was definitley feeling a sense of joy and relief all at the same time.

Jesse let a few minutes pass. Joe needed a quick break. Jesse gave him time to let it all soak in as if he knew what may be coming next.

Joe inhaled a large breath of fresh air. His question seemed innocent. "I feel like I've always believed. I mean, since I was a kid, I've always believed."

Joe knew the correct answer was coming, just from Jesse's smile. "But somewhere along the way the communication fell off. It fell away. Slipped to the back-burner."

After a quick pause, Jesse added dejectedly, "and for some, it was never really established. Not real communication. Not life-enriching communication."

Jesse continued, "You need to move forward now; that's the next step. You already established that you believe. Communication. Moving forward. That's the next step. God is smiling at you and is desiring for you to move forward.... Communicate with Him. That's the next step. Actually, Joe, it's the only step. All else will follow. But first, we must communicate".

Joe agreed, "I want to move forward. I want to... communicate."

Jesse leaned up to add impact to his next statement. He looked deep into Joe's eyes. The stillness of the mid-morning seemed to sweep Joe to another place entirely. There was not a sound within the house or outside. Joe anxiously awaited Jesse's next words.

"Read.... Pray.... Worship.... Believe."

Silence again for a few seconds.

Huh?

"Read. Pray. Worship. Believe." Again, Jesse offered the seemingly simple commands.

"You see, that's where your free will and God's plans for you come together."

'For I know the plans that I have for you,' declares the LORD, ran through Joe's mind. *The verse from Jeremiah that he told me about....*

"Continually seek God.... How? Communicate.... How? Read, pray, worship, and believe."

"**Read** His word and books that enriches your understanding and thus enriches you."

"**Pray** to Him. Not just your list of requests, but talk to Him. YES, talk to Him. And most of all, thank Him continually."

"**Worship** Him.... Yes, at church services, but most importantly, every day. Consume your thoughts about Him and about your reading."

"If you do this, the Spirit of God will lead you. Then believe God is speaking to you. AND, if you do believe, then put belief in action and do what you are led to do."

"**Believe** continually that He is guiding you. Even when things may not seem good, or actually are bad, still believe that He is in control of you and your well-being.... ALWAYS."

"Think of it this way.... Faith equals praise continually"

Jesse saw Joe's mind racing.

"Faith means complete confidence and trust.... And continually means without ceasing...."

That's almost hard to understand... but... is so simple to say. I feel like I can do that.... I want to do that.

Jesse continued. "This past week, you have earnestly started this.... Read John 6, verses 28 and 29. Doing the work of God is believing in the Son.... Read it.... And believing invokes action, right? Reading, praying, worshiping.... And most of all, don't let it just be something you DO... BECOME IT. Become as one with the Word and live a fulfilled life on your journey."

"It's not intended for you to do life alone. Jesus has come. He came to earth, stepped into our worldly mess, to carry us through it; whatever troubles we have, to carry us out of it, and into a better life."

Silence filled the air again and Joe gazed in deep thought. A few seconds later, Jesse continued.

"Each has their own journey, Joe. All unique.... Unique, Joe.... You get that? A unique journey for each.... You think God created man to live simple, unfulfilled, repetitive, boring lives? That all we're supposed to do is sit on a church pew and occasionally do a task around the church; ho-hum...." Jesse rolled his eyes to add emphasis and paused to get Joe's reaction.

Joe took a break from his gaze and focused his attention on Jesse again. *He knows I'm soaking this up. That I'm desperate for answers. How much does he know about me?* Then the wise old man continued discipling his pupil.

"A relationship with God is solely personal. If our earthly lives were not meant to be fascinating and challenging... adventurous... don't you think the Bible would have a few pages listing out exact courses of action for all of us to repeat?" Jesse sat back in his chair and bit his bottom lip in anticipation of the rest of his dissertation. Then he continued.

"Have you ever wondered why practically all of Christ's teachings seem so vague, especially to non-believers? Or even to new believers. Or that the verses seem so simple? When in reality, their meanings are deep. And as you grow in Christ... through reading, praying, worshiping... and doing... they get even deeper... and deeper.... And there is no finish line Joe. There is NO ultimate plateau to reach as a Christian. Not on earth. We constantly grow. Therefore, your understanding gets deeper and deeper into the Bible, as it specifically relates to you.... To you.... Specifically to you, and your journey."

Jesse paused again, then continued.

"Earth life is a journey. Regardless of your faith, or belief, or depth of following or understanding; it's still a journey. No one can deny that; that it truly is a journey. God's desire is to give us our full blessings on this journey. The blessings he has for each of us. Blessings in all areas of our life... and understand, blessings are 'gifts bestowed by God; the invocation of God's favor upon a person'. We have to desire it and grow in Him." Then he briefly paused again and Joe waited earnestly. "To give life and have it more abundantly.... You ever heard that Joe?"

Like a humbled child, Joe acknowledged, "Yes".

Then Jesse continued. "How can we start receiving our full blessings? Our calling?"

Joe stared further into Jesse's eyes as if the answer was buried deep inside. *How?*

"Huh? How can we?" Jesse asked and then waited a few seconds, his hand resting on Joe's shoulder. Before answering his own question, he gently shook him.

"Read. Pray. Worship. Believe."

Joe thought and then started to speak. Jesse could see him forming questions but Joe couldn't put the words together. He tried to stumble through it.

"Uh, okay... I see. We believe and we desire God's will on our life... but... tell me...how.... I mean, give me... or can you give me a real-life example....."

"Of course!"

"I mean, like for me, in my life. I just work a simple job; have a simple home... just kind of ordinary. Am I supposed to think that I'm supposed to be a missionary or preacher or something?"

Jesse gave a reassuring chuckle. "Think of it this way, Joe…. You have free will to pursue whatever you want…. Free will…. God allows everyone free will. He doesn't impose anything on anyone. Let's say, for instance, that someone is not happy and satisfied in life. Like their life is, well, like yours has been, then what should they do?" Jesse paused knowing a response may not be coming.

Then he continued, "they should do something about it. They should change something and begin a pursuit of their desires. Action invokes results. No action, well…."

"I see."

"If living for God is your top priority and you are actively doing that, then simply pursue your desires, without ever letting it become more important than fervently desiring to grow closer to the Lord. So, regardless of what your likes and interests are, simply make pursuing God your first priority… and how do you do that?"

Joe smiled and answered, "Read, pray, worship, believe".

Jesse chuckled, "ring the bell, we have a winner". They both laughed before he continued, "so, by making God first priority; all else will sort of… fall in line…."

Joe knew this was another revelation. *This one trumps the others. It's all coming together.*

Before he let him surmise too much, Jesse reminded him, "but still life is challenging…. There are always challenges….

And yes, there's heartache too. There's things we must go through to make us what we are to be... make us stronger, but there's also, well... bad things."

Jesse's student listened intently for the next revelation. He wanted this one badly. *Why does God let bad things happen to us? Why...*

Jesse continued and interrupted his thought. "Remember free will, Joe?"

Yeah.

"Well, that means people are free to serve God and also free to not serve God. Right?"

Yeah....

"You know John 3:16, right?"

Joe nodded.

"He loved the world, it says.... Loved the world.... And whosoever believes in the Son.... Will not perish but have everlasting life. The point missed so often is that God loves us all; all of us; the world. Believers and non-believers alike. It doesn't say that God loved the ones that one day would believe on his Son, does it?"

Joe shook his head in agreement.

"It's not up to us to figure out how God loves even the evil doers. Not the sin, but the evil doer. Perhaps understanding love that deep is unattainable for humans? But we are instructed to love everyone... and especially our enemies. And know this Joe;

if we always put God first, and continually thank and praise him.... You catch that Joe? Always... in everything. In every trial, battle, challenge, etcetera, on and on, day in, day out... then God WILL make good out of EVERY thing that comes our way.... Remember, all we are supposed to do is trust in that next step.... We are not to fret about the entire path. Or let's say journey". Jesse smiled and leaned back in his chair again.

"Let me ask you this, Joe", the teacher continued. "We naturally agree that 'bad' things happen to us... that heartaches sometimes come our way... that overwhelming challenges sometimes come our way. Yet, God wants us to make Him center of our lives... our light unto our path.... If that's true, then shouldn't we just keep talking to God, all the way through whatever disaster we are in at the time?" Jesse paused. "Didn't Jesus go off by Himself to pray? To talk to the Father.... He went into the mountains. He went deep into the garden. Remember; Christian equals Christ-like. The savior prayed for direction and understanding and most of all; God's will be done. You think you should do the same?"

That revelation caused Joe to gaze blankly for a few seconds. *Wow. That is amazing.* Joe knew of the scripture Jesse referred to and knew he had read it and heard it before. *I've never realized this. This is like a... whole new understanding.*

"But, don't be fooled. God is not a genie in a lamp that we rub from time to time to get what we want. Striving to keep

Him center of our life... that is the goal. And unfortunately, we fail many times, but He IS always there.... Always."

Joe began to smile and joyful tears filled his eyes. His voice softly whimpered as he tried to speak. 'Amazing Love' sang in his thoughts as he thought about the many times he had forgotten God; the many times he had ignored what he new was right.

Before he got too carried away in his emotions, Jesse returned to the question Joe had posed a few minutes before.

"Examples, right?" Jesse said.

Joe's breath quivered as he sat more upright and breathed in to catch his breath. *What example?*

"Real life examples, I think is how you put it."

The statement brought Joe's attention fully to his mentor, as he looked at him again.

"God is to be exemplified and magnified in all walks of life, or functions of life, so to speak, on this planet. Think of the doctor that gives God credit publicly after a life is saved. Or what about the fireman or paramedic that acknowledges God's hand in rescuing someone. How about this? What about the shoe salesman that shares God's goodness to customers daily? Through actual word or sometimes just through kindness and neighborly love. What about the business person that receives advancement in their job and anonymously shares their monetary increases with people in need."

After a brief pause, Jesse continued.

"What about the coach that has a passion for the sport but puts God first and interjects Godly principles into how he conducts himself. What an impact that makes! Possibly on a young person that has no Godly influence at home. Amazing isn't it Joe? How God is really everywhere; in everything, if people will let Him be. How about the professional athlete that many adore and look up to, that let's Christ shine in their life and publicly, truly, thanks God. All of these people are doing what they love and are passionate about and they let God direct their life."

Joe wiped his eyes and sniffed. He was joyous for all the revelations that were being revealed to him.

"Joe, this is what the world needs to hear.... This is what they need to hear. The people need to hear it. Real life stories. Stories of people living their daily lives with God as their director; instructor, and striving to let Christ shine in their lives.... You know, the Church that Christ is returning for does not consist of mortar and brick...."

After letting that statement sink in a few seconds, Jesse added, "do you think God calls us to be church goers?"

After another short pause, he continued, "does that sound odd? Don't be confused at this point."

The comment caused Joe to squint his eyes in deep thought.

"Just think about it. We're called to seek, find, and live God's calling upon our lives. Church, as most think of it, should not be the focus of one's journey, but yet church should be far more valuable in people's lives than what most allow it to be. Ya get what I'm saying? A journey to God, with God, is about much more than most understand. Don't you think that if people desired God first, then church positions, jobs, functions, missions, etcetera, would flourish.... As people simply desired to follow God first, always."

Jesse saw the bewildered expression in front of him and paused again before finishing. "Church may cease to appear as we currently know it if more people began realizing this. Church would be a lot more. In fact, a great spiritual awakening may even take place...." Jesse chuckled an all knowing laugh to himself, then continued.

"Remember, Christiananity is a personal journey, unique to each, but yet at the core, is same for all; to spread the Gospel and make disciples. The common baseline for all believers is for each to read, pray, worship, and believe. Four simple little words, but much deeper.... Read. Pray. Worship. Believe. Kind of like your revelations; you experienced Bible passages that society has deemed to be just simple children's stories, but yet you discovered revelations for your life as they leaped from the pages.... And now life is starting to be clearer for you; your abyss is disappearing, isn't it?"

Jesse continued to talk but Joe's mind slowly drifted. Something didn't sound right. *I understand and agree with everything he's saying. I believe it.... That Church, as in Christ's Church that he is returning for is about individual people coming to know him and live their lives as He leads. Not about tens of thousands of individual 'church' buildings....* Joe shook his head as if to remove the oddity of whatever Jesse had said that didn't sound right.

But something just... is odd. Joe's eyes drifted away from Jesse and his joyful expression became blank. He could not shake the feeling that despite the numerous, wonderful revelations he's being gifted with, that something just isn't right.

What is it? What is so odd about what he said? I can't.... Bewilderment returned full bore. Jesse was still talking but Joe wasn't listening anymore. Like a contestant struggling to find the right answer to a trivia question, Joe tensed up and squinted his eyes in deep thought.

Then it hit him suddenly; the answer he desired. Except maybe not the answer he wanted to hear. The day had been bizarre enough without this; without the discovery that just reached up and smacked him right on the cheek.

How? How can this be?

The realization of what was odd and strange startled him. Despite the glorious teachings of his grandpa friend that caused so many revelations, Joe was now moving from startled to frightened. He began searching his thoughts and memory in a futile attempt to disprove what suddenly hit him.

I haven't told him... he thought, then slowly shifted his eyes back to the teacher sitting in front of him, *about my abyss.... I never did tell him. I never did refer to my problem as an abyss.* His mind shifted back to his dismal thought at the lake nearly a week ago. The one word description that summed up his emptiness.

Abyss. That's what I called my problem. That's the word that seemed to fit. That's what I called it last weekend, standing by the water. Without warning, he returned to the scene. He pictured himself standing only a few feet from the lake that nestled at the foot of the mountain range. As if he had changed channels, he switched from sitting at a table to holding a fishing rod and tackle box. The mysterious morning and miriade of thoughts and emotions somehow disappeared. Miraculously, these feelings vanished. Perhaps beauty of the surroundings filled the void left by rapidly departing stress and bewilderment.

Trees waved an orange glow as a gentle breeze blew. Not to be outdone, an array of red and yellow leaves beckoned for his admiration as they joined in. Pines and cedar trees offered their mix of green needles. Together, the fall foliage that consumed him provided a quite solitude. Though his mind replayed the abyssmal thoughts brought on by Jesse's reference, Joe was eager to bask in the beauty of God's creation as he tried to recapture the essence he medially flirted with only a few days before.

So much more beautiful, he thought, as he compared his memory with how it now appeared in his mind's eye. He wished he could really be there to enjoy it as he should have done before. *The mountains; they're more strikingly vivid than I realized last week.* Trees blanketed the mountain side with a colorful cascade. The utmost reaches of the peak had already given in to winter's call and only a few leaves remained, leaving empty branches to sway. Barren limbs were grey and desolate on the trees near the top. *It's like I can see every detail of each tree branch.* As gentle breezes blew, the limbs seem to wave goodbye.

Joe enjoyed his return to the lake. Like the cover of a November issue of Southern Living, the surroundings were an image to behold. It seemed as though the fresh, crisp air was actually filling his lungs with each breath. A fish jumped, causing ripples, and interrupted his gaze. His focus shifted from the mountains to the broken mirrored image of the water laying before him. As if the creatures wanted to compete for their share of his attention, a frog leaped into the water in front of him. The splash won and he lowered his head as he retreated his stare from the fish's ripple to the frog's display, only a few feet in front of him. As he looked into the water, he wondered why he didn't see his reflection.

The grass was browning from summer's passing. In awe of the vivid memory, he shifted his weight to the side, scuffled his foot, and caused a subtle crunch of blades beneath his feet. All his senses were flush with details. Autumn breezes caused rustling leaves and the fragrances of fall filled his nose. The level of peacefulness brought on by his vivid recall may have been greater than if he had actually been present. His memory waited for him to move on. The sun had now lowered beneath the horizon causing a quandary of decision. Should he force his mind's eye to continue on; to turn and retrace his steps back to the woods, just as he had done previously, or to relenquish his grasp on his recall, or to just stand and steal every second possible from the scene until all light was gone? Trepidation grew into deeper concern. Without realizing it, he had turned and faced the woods. The hill that led back to the edge of the woods was before him. The quick jump in his recall tried to tell him that this was only his mind's replay of previous events. He had not turned himself to leave. He wasn't sure if he should acknowledge it, but it was like an invisible hand was gently pressing on his back, telling him it was okay to go ahead and climb the gradual incline to the forest's edge.

The light was fading. I had to get going. I didn't conciously.... He hesitated in his thoughts.... *Or subconciously? turn to leave.* He wanted to look back at the autumn scene one more time, to enjoy the beauty as he should have when he was actually there, but instead he was suddenly stricken by his next thought. He quickly shook his head in an attempt to erase the line of thought. Somewhere, deep in his brain a bad thought formed. A bad, scary thought. A thought brought on by the recall. One that he didn' t want to acknowledge. The gentle enticing hand continued to urge him. The growing darkness accentuated the looming thought. He couldn't make himself overcome it. He began to accept that this lakeshore recall was only a transient phase.

Jesse!

Conscious focus was unattainable. He wanted to return to his kitchen table and rejoin Jesse's teachings. Shaking his head and blinking rapidly didn't work. He quickly gave in and stopped trying.

No.

He tried to reason. He tried to beg.

No. Please, no! His thoughts cried. He began to weep. His face became taught as he readied himself for the climax of the thought that was pressing. The thought that was sadly pressing into full fruition. The gentle presence urged from behind. He whimpered. His eyelids squeezed tightly together but tears pierced through.

I don't want to leave them, he thought in broken fragments as weeping turned to crying. His chest pained. The pressing thought was revealing itself.

I love them. Oh, God..., how I love them. Snapshots of his children jumped before him. A cheeleader leaped and cheered. A football game played behind her. *My doll. My sweetheart.* As quickly as he consumed the image, the next appeared. One after another. Seemingly faster than comprehensible, the images came. His children, just as he last saw them. Streamers hung from the ceiling, draped from each corner of the room to the adjacent corner. The family sang Happy Birthday. He wanted to jump into the picture and be a part of it. Thousands of images streamed by, yet he somehow consumed each one as they transitioned from still to a short movie. Some memories he knew. Others required dislodging by the snapshot as it appeared. Regardless, all were his memories.

Christmas presents tore open and the little one jumped with joy as the toy was pulled from the box.

The ball barely trickled off the tee as she threw her bat down and ran. She was the tiniest player, but she pumped her legs like the fastest on the team.

She looked up at her mom, just tall enough to see the stovetop and asked, can I help mom?

The puppy delighted in her love and licked her smiling face as she laughed and rolled her head from side to side to avoid a doggy kiss on the lips. The images kept coming.

Sadness. He weeped, whimpered and cried. Heartbreak. *How did I forget all this? Why now do I realize this?* The images continued. The thought was now reality. No more question to it. *This is how it happens...?*

His wife stood at the back of the church as the congregation rose to their feet. He heard the music and behind the vail, she started down the aisle.

Their first car pulled into the drive. The small, sparingly-furnished apartment welcomed them.

The scenes kept coming.

Mom! Dad! Other images of his life were now rolling by. His heart cried out in a mix of hurt and desire, *I want to see them.* Images of him and his dad flashed by. He thought of the good and bad times. The things he wished he had said. And things he wished he hadn't. He saw them going for their first drive, when he sat up high in the seat and followed the instructions. He saw grandpa; smiling and waving.

There's mom; cooking. They're all there. He longed to join them. To put himself in each one. To lavish in the warmth and happiness. To be there one more time. To have a chance to do it over. To enjoy every single second of every single memory.

Scene after scene swept by. High school friends, family members long forgotten; page after page of memory; replaying every second of his life. Nothing was missing. Time seemed to no longer exist. The images raced by, yet he enjoyed reflections of each one; even simple things.

That bike. I painted it myself. Not longer after I learned to ride.

Ah, Ms. Walker; My Sunday school teacher. She was so good to me.

Somehow, pain and anguish had subsided. His tears had stopped flowing. The gentle, reassuring nudge from behind was now encircling him and aided in his ease of heartache.

The scenes continued and he didn't miss a single moment of his life. He saw images that were not capable in life. *That's what mom and dad looked like*! Images were now racing that depicted things he had only seen in photo albums. His parents in his early childhood. A toddler played while they watched. The innocent child muttered happy requests as they looked down at him. His sippy cup in hand and toy in the other. The chair his dad sat in had long been forgotten, yet he recalled it vividly; his young dad, in that old chair; the feel, the design, the wore out cushion. He saw a young man and woman, full of life; vibrant; their whole life in front of them. He thought of how lively they looked and longed for that image to stay. This image and not the one from a few years later when he was by their bedside. When he had to let them go when their time came.

Whimpering and crying had stopped. Acceptance of this point of his journey had set in. The thought was no longer a thought. It was real.

I never came out of those woods.

His time had come.

The woods he had entered last Saturday that would lead him to his car and ultimately home had never released him. He had never returned home from his afternoon of fishing. The past week, the 'dreams', must have all been his mind's attempt to carry on as his breathing faded.

Heart attack? He wondered, in regards to his death.

Thoughts of what might have been the rest of his life rose up and quickly subsided. He started to cry but no tears came.

The forgone opportunity to cherish life had ended.

Did they find me yet? He wondered, in regards to his body.

CHAPTER 11

THERAPY

Therapists sometimes say the best way to get relief from depression is to go to sleep. That's all. Just go to sleep. Give your soul a chance to unwind, refresh and start over. Thousands of books have been written about how to achieve a better life. How to overcome struggles. How to make a better you. How to reach your dreams. The key fact that sums it all up, that is the center of every book; that is at the core of every therapy session; that is the first requirement, is that the afflicted person has to be willing to change. It's up to that individual to decide to pick themselves up. It's up to that person to change their direction. It's up to that person to decide to listen to the therapist. It's up to that person to pursue the teachings of the self-improvement book. It's up to that person to seek a better life; to reach for their dreams. It's up to that person to decide to live life to the fullest.

It's up to that person to decide to simply go to sleep, so to speak, wake up, and start over again.

Joe had suffered through the latter part of his young life. Bearing depression had robbed him of potential joy. Joy of simply sharing each day with his precious family. Joy of simply standing by the water's edge and taking in the beauty of God's creation.

Joe had let himself get off track of the true pleasures of life. He realized this when it was almost too late.

"Joe".

The voice called again, "Joe".

They sat motionless. Not a sound broke the silence. A glimmer of hope sprang to life in the sound of heartbeat pounding in his ears. His eyes popped open and they stared at each other. Not a word was spoken. Sweat beaded on his forehead. His heartbeat raced in his ears. They sat, just as they had at the table, facing each other.

Another chance!!!!

Jesse smiled. Joe exhaled.

Breathe!

Joe blinked his eyes, then squeezed his hands and released them. He wanted to feel movement; to know that he was alive.

Another chance!!!!

Jesse raised his brow slightly and tilted his head back as if to say, 'uh-huh', thought you might want another go at it.

Visions of his family and his life showered his thoughts. Joe began to smile. He chuckled in delight. He smiled even bigger.

Another chance!!!!

Joe relished in the new opportunity. Before he could form another thought, Jesse placed his hand on Joe's heart. Joe slowly looked down at it and then back up. Jesse peered deep into Joe's eyes. Jesse still smiled convincingly and Joe knew all was okay.

Then his loving, grandpa-figure friend smiled even bigger and gently pushed him.

Immediately Joe awoke. He breathed in deeply. His eyes opened wide. He didn't feel odd or weird or bewildered. The expression on his face confirmed how he felt, and more importantly it confirmed what suddenly consumed him; completeness, fulfillment, joy, and victory. He lay motionless in his bed. His bed. In his house. He didn't want to move before he could collect himself and confirm that he was in fact in his bed, in his home.

Soft, he thought as he squeezed the sheets. He peered around the room. Early daylight was peeping through the drapes and revealed that everything was in order. He was home, in his bed, and he was positive.

Potential questions tried to surface but he was able to ignore them. He was happy. He was relieved. He was refreshed. He wouldn't let them form before removing them from his thoughts. He considered trying to determine what day it was, then decided against it. He was happy.

He sat up. As many details as he had experienced in the dream, he realized there is no mistaking the details of really waking up in your bed in your home. He checked his senses. Smelled like home. Felt like home. Looked like home.

He turned on the lamp and grabbed a notebook and pen from the nightstand. Scooting back to lean against the headboard, he realized his wife was beside him resting peacefully. A sense of assuredness joined his bliss as he softly reached out and touched her. *Dear, we have so much to talk about.... You just... don't... know how much.* He was happy again.

Confidence in re-kindling their relationship managed to win out over his parallel thought of, *is today Friday?* He thought of the roses that he was sending to her work.

Or was that just in the dream? The question caused him to smile because it reassured him that his thrill ride was over and it was time to wake up and move on with his new life.

There was no desire to expand any further thought on answering the question as to which day he had awoke to. He was consumed with joy. He knew the most important topic had been addressed.... The abyss was closed and he was sure of it.

Purpose and completeness filled him. *Continue reading, praying, worshiping, and believing, and all will fall in line.* He heard Jesse's words again and assured himself that this was the instruction for guiding his life.

The smile he woke with somehow grew larger, then his eyes widened with excitement as he remembered Jesse's instructions... *Joe, this is what the world needs to hear....*

He said it to himself again, *Joe, this is what the world needs to hear! This is what they need to hear....*

He asked himself, *does God want me to be a....*

Wonder if He's calling me to....

He shook his head and smiled confidently; knowing that there will be time to discover those revelations later.

He knew the most important purpose for him right now....

He opened the notebook. His very essence burned with determination to tell others; to help others; to help the world. As the pen reached the paper, he realized the entire encounter was as vivid as watching a movie. A tear of joy rolled down his cheek.

The pen flowed effortlessly across the paper as he began recording his journey thus far....

The sun hovered above the mountains and the lake was peacefully still....

THE END

Summary

This sums up my experience after I asked God to show me He was real.

"I experienced periods of affinity with God. I would lie on my bedroom floor, reading my Bible, going at the words for hours, all of them strong like arms wrapped tightly around my chest. It seemed as though the words were alive with minds and motions of their own, as though God were crawling thought inside my head for guidance, comfort, and strength."

From <u>Blue Like Jazz</u>, by Donald Miller.

Unfortunately, it took deep, severe, suicidal depression for me to stumble into the start of this 'marriage'.

I'm passionate to tell people how to escape from hell on earth, (depression), and encourage everyone that the 'marriage' is without a doubt, the very best life we can live on this planet.

"There is a time when every person who encounters Jesus, who believes Jesus is the Son of God, decides that they will spend their life following Him. Some people, like the Apostle Paul, make this decision the minute they become a Christian. Others, like the Apostle Peter, endure years of half-hearted commitment and spiritual confusion before leaping in with all their passion. Still others may enjoy some benefits of God's love and grace without entering into true joy of marriage with their maker."

From <u>Blue Like Jazz</u>, by Donald Miller.

Note from author...

Hopefully, since you are reading this section, it indicates you were moved or touched somewhat by Joe's story; that part or all of your own journey can relate to Joe. Or at least you understand Joe's struggles and despair. Maybe his story just simply entertained you enough to prompt questions. Or perhaps, you are intrigued enough to get a deeper glimpse of what the writer was trying to convey.

The fact is, that regardless of where you are; regardless of your age; regardless of your gender; regardless of what is happening to you and around you; regardless of the life you live, there is one certain fact that is true for every person. There is a God. And there is a Christ. And there is a Holy Spirit.

And since there is a Supreme Deity, then, possibly, there is some part of you, that is like me, that has tried to ask Him the question; "is this it? Is this really what life is all about? Is this really how life is supposed to be?"

Maybe you can't fully relate to that tirade of questions. Maybe things are great for you. Perhaps you are living the 'American dream'. Or....

Maybe it's like Joe; full of dread and despair. Or maybe, like most, it lies somewhere in between -?

Regardless of where your answer lands on the spectrum of thought, would you at least agree that it is a fair question - 'Is this really how life is supposed to be?'

If you've reached this part of the book and you believe your life is as good as it can possibly be; that there is no way to be more fulfilled; more rewarded, more happier, and you're never burdened with a struggle, then thank you for reading and put the book away.

For the rest of us, whether dealing with despair or desiring greater fulfillment, take it a step further. If you believe in a Supreme Deity, an all powerful, all knowing God, and you are willing to accept that He is all loving and wants to bless us, then you have to be at least open to the idea that He wants to communicate this to us. If you're still willing to continue this thought, then be willing to consider His forms of communication.

Consider Joe's revelations; simple yet profound. Four easy instructions: read, pray, worship, believe.

Before continuing with Joes' revelations, consider this: Christ delivered man from ritualistic tasks and rules. Christ created a direct link with God; a way for every person to know God through Christ. You may already know this, like I did, but still are brave enough to ask, "Is this it? Is this really how life is supposed to be?" I'm glad that in my pit of despair I was brave enough to ask it, and furthermore to say, "then show me God".

And so began the next step of my journey. I started finding peace, relief, comfort, and joy as I started realizing what the Bible is. The more I longed for God to show me, the more entranced I became in His Word. Just as Joe, I realized that the Bible is simple and profound at the same time. I had finally discovered that the Bible really is our source for guidance in life. The more I read, the more direction (and happiness, and assuredness, and fulfillment) I received. The Bible is simple stories and simple instructions and at the same time it's profound, dynamic, life-enriching revelations. I can't attempt to relay it because as Jesse points out, it's revelations and life's answers pertains to each of us in our own unique journey.

It had finally hit me; the most profound revelation of all; His Book has to be this way. Simple and profound. How else could it relate to every unique journey on the planet? Every person, every journey, all unique. We're all different and all at different steps on our journey. I fully accepted what the Bible is intended to be and realized that all aspects of desiring God's direction for me falls under the umbrella of four simple words; read, pray, worship, believe. We have to open up the communication lines with God.

Try it for yourself. Before that though, do you love God? Do you believe that Christ was sacrificed for atonement for all man's sins, and was raised from the dead? If so, then close your eyes and tell Him in your mind that you believe it and that He is Lord. Now get a Bible and read Romans chapter 9, verses 9 and 10. Even if you've done this before, do it again. Then read John chapter 3, verses 16 and 17.

> 16 "For God so loved the world, that He gave His only begotten Son, that whosoever believes in Him shall not perish, but have eternal life.
> 17 "For God did not send the Son into the world to judge the world, but that the world might be saved through Him.

If you've never done this, then do it earnestly, sincerely, and let the compelling of your heart lead you to say, "I accept you Jesus as my savior". If you just accepted Christ, then go find a pastor or a Christian friend, and tell them.

Then, go live your life. Life is going to happen regardless. Now you can face it with Christ leading the way for you.

Pursue your interests; pursue you dreams, while desiring to grow closer to God (read, pray, worship, believe). This results in ultimate happiness and fulfillment.

Pursue interest and desire God = fulfillment.

For example, a person that loves motorcycles starting or joining a biker church. Check out FreedomBikerChurchGreenville. com.

Or a person that loves dirt track racing and gives out Bibles at dirt track races. Check out "The Dirt Racers Bible" at Dirt racing outreach in Knoxville, TN. Also check out DirtracingforJesus.com.

Or an avid outdoorsmen or hunter using their passion as a platform for promoting God's word. Check out MichaelLordoutdoors.com.

How about a pro football player writing books about their walk with God. Check out Shaun Alexander's Touchdown Alexander or The Walk.

What about Tim Tebow's public acknowledgment of his love for God?

Read some of Joe Gibbs' books. A coach and race team owner telling of his relationship with God.

For understanding the dire need of being a light of the nation and leading a return to God, read <u>The Harbinger</u>, by Jonathan Cahn.

For a unique understanding of God's love and mercy, read <u>The Shack</u>, by William Paul Young.

For a renewed charge in life, read, <u>Unleash!; Breaking Free From Normalcy</u>, by Perry Noble.

For desiring true contentment and happiness, read <u>Unexplainable</u>, by Don Cousins.

For wisdom and insight, read <u>Dying to Live</u> by Clayton King.

Find your own examples. Discover countless other books. There are thousands and thousands of examples of people living a fulfilled life by pursing God's will for their life.

Most of all, the greatest examples are in your Bible. Read it. Pray to God. Worship Him. And Believe.

Life is happening, regardless. Make it fulfilling; take the next step on your journey.

The Journey

Acknowledgments

I seldom read this section in books, because they usually say the same thing; thanks, thanks, thanks. But now I realize it is so true! So many people to thank in order to make a book a reality. Way too many to possibly list all and not risk leaving someone out. With apologies to so many people I will accidentally not include, I will try to give thanks.

God, first of course! Then the loves of my life; Michele, Chelsea, Christa. Wow, so amazed everyday that someone as undeserving as me can be blessed with 3 amazing people! Whether playing in the dirt or writing a book, their support is full of love and very powerful. Thank you.

All 3 sets of my parents, extended family, friends, mentors, life advisors, pastors, church family and others. I love you all and thank God for each of you. The 'TV room and Grill 41' friends are what happiness is all about! Thank you.

Kellie Frazier and DayOfLove.org is the ignition for putting this book in motion. You are a special and talented lady. Too many individual things to thank you for, like standing in the care room for over an hour and listening to my passion for this book. Thank you.

Mom, your beautiful painting made an amazingly awesome book cover. I used to look at it in your house and picture Joe standing in it long before anyone knew there was a book. All of your paintings are beautiful. Thank you for being a mom full of love and support… and for letting me use your painting.

Stefano Fontana is an awesome designer, site developer and person. Thank you for all the hard work and for decoding what I try to say and making it come alive.

Taylor McCullough and Jamie Hughes – your work on editing this book is remarkable. You spent a lot of time on it and I'm beyond grateful. Everyone that is impacted by it owes a thanks to you for making it readable. There were 'Landrumisms' to fix! Many laughs! Wow, is all I can say in regards to support you gave. Thank you is simply not enough. I pray God's blessings on you and desire to show my thanks in a greater way!

Stacy, you are a beautiful, wonderful supporter, mentor, friend, and confidant. I experienced a lot with you, like at my kitchen table and on the many Rex ministry trips to Duke

University Hospital. Thank you for everything. I desire to express gratitude in greater ways.

Erin, John, and everyone else that helped edit or pre-read, thank you! Wouldn't have gotten off the ground without you!

Sherberts, you are a blessing! Thankful for your support in many ways — still proud of the tilework! Your expertise in video production is amazing! Many thanks!

Thank you to several coffee shops and restaurants, but especially to Southern Delights. This book was completed in your shop and it's fitting it was launched and celebrated there. Many thanks!

Heath

P.S.
(Practical Steps that I learned)

While letting Jesus re-shape me, I had to make changes of my own. I desired God's help in my habits, practices, routines, social life, interests, etc.

I learned that it's about steps. I didn't just embrace Hope and Desire and suddenly step out of depression, (D). I also had painful reminders along the way that 'fake bliss' set me up for hurt. I like the term 'cautiously aggressive'. Growth by leaps and bounds sometimes created instability for me. So, the lesson was that I should be 'in control' of my 'happy' emotions as well.

The 'fuel' for my Hope and Desire came (still comes) from Jesus. He is truly the answer to everything for me. Aligning my life with Him didn't mean I became "churchy" or "religious". To me, these kind of people can be so fake that it's sickening. They seem to focus on a perception of perfection. For me, Jesus made me more confidant of who I am. Made me more real. This was accomplished by communicating with Him though READING, PRAYING, WORSHIPPING, AND BELIEVING. It started with many small steps, kind of like learning to walk. After I 'crawled' in the Word, I built steam to the point of marathon running. I truly believe Jesus is the best 'fuel' for my life and everyone else's.

READ. PRAY. WORSHIP. BELIEVE.

<u>Consider this:</u>

Jeremiah 29:11 says God has a plan for me.

1Corithians 15:57 says I have victory through Jesus Christ.

John 10:10 says that He wants to give me abundant life.

Philipians 4:13 says I can do anything with Jesus.

Acts 1:8 says by accepting Jesus, I have accessible power.

All of these verses are great when everything is going along fine but life can still suck sometime! So, I also believe these verses.

Romans 8:28 says everything works out to my good because I love the Lord.

James 1:2-4 says I should be joyous when crap comes my way because it's how God shapes me to be what He wants me to be, which is definitely my best life. (remember Jeremiah 29:11).

<u>So how do I cope with crap?</u>

Proverbs 3:5-6 says to not try to figure it all out, but just trust in Jesus.

<u>So what do I do when I truly consume these verses but still 'feel bad'?</u>

I do something I enjoy. Like home projects, reading, watching sports, going to the coffee shop, or just sitting on the deck. Sometimes, I take a nap.

Yep, that's how you do it!

www.ingramcontent.com/pod-product-compliance
Lightning Source LLC
Chambersburg PA
CBHW021332190726
48288CB00003B/1077